THE REBEL'S CUPID

LOVE'S MAGIC BOOK 2

NIKI MITCHELL

This is a work of fiction. Names, characters, places and incidents are the product of the author's imagination or are used fictitiously. Any resemblance to actual persons living or dead, business establishments, events, or location is entirely coincidental. This publisher does not have any control and does not assume responsibility for author or third-party website or their content.

Printed in the United States of America

❀ Created with Vellum

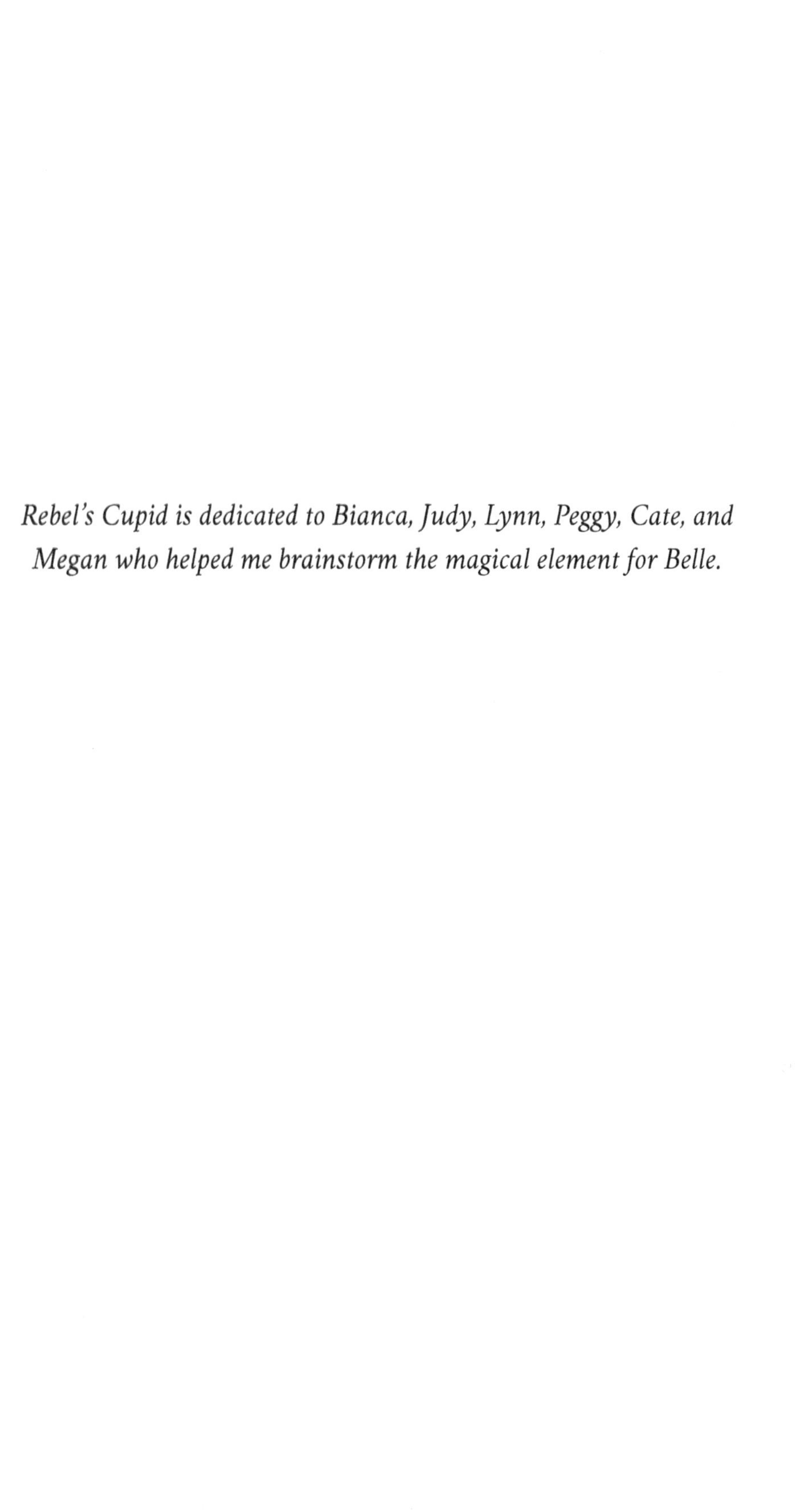

Rebel's Cupid is dedicated to Bianca, Judy, Lynn, Peggy, Cate, and Megan who helped me brainstorm the magical element for Belle.

UNTITLED

REBEL'S CUPID

Curiosity didn't kill the Cupid …
it just got Belle Brooks in a whole heap of trouble.

Belle Brooks, a red-headed Cupid, ventures into the forbidden human world looking for her aunt. She finds a gorgeous hunk of a biker who's off-limits because he's mortal (gasp). She should stay away, except he's just the man to help her handle the shocking family secret her trip to earth has revealed.

Lucky O'Sullivan can't believe it. For once, he might be as fortunate as his name implies. A stunning redhead just walked into his bar. Turns out, she's just as handy with a wrench as she is hot, and that pushes all of his buttons. Small problem … he just got dumped and isn't sure his heart can handle Belle.

Enjoy this modern love story with a light paranormal twist.

CHAPTER 1

Realm of Cupid's Corner

BELLE BROOKS LONGED to see the world—not flutter along Forest Avenue on her way to work.

She should have been content with her town's beautiful setting, suspended above puffy cumulus clouds and nestled between majestic snowcapped mountains. She should have been content living close to the grassy meadows surrounding Lake Aphrodite. She should have been soothed as she breathed in fresh air, resplendent with the scent of poppies, lupines, pansies, zinnias, and pink lady slippers.

She should have been content.

Nevertheless, she wasn't. If anything, her yearnings for an

adventure far from the confines of this community grew stronger with each breath. Too bad only the most accurate Cupid archers visited Earth to shoot arrows and infuse humans with love. Since Belle couldn't hit the side of a castle, she was stuck here. It just didn't seem fair.

Fate gifted her with a high IQ. She appreciated being smart, but that didn't stop her from longing for more.

Veering onto Paramour Street, she glanced at the clock tower. At ten minutes to nine, she'd better flutter faster. If she didn't hurry, she'd be late. Her promotion to Innovative Productions took two years to get. She was not about to blow it today.

Zooming past Cupid's Daily Press and the high school, she arrived at Truelove Headquarters. An enormous six-foot Cupid statue dominated the front entrance of the white four-story building. She glided toward a bow-and-arrow icon on the wall and waved her heart-shaped wrist emblem at the sensor. A coral-pink light flashed, and the cloud-covered door parted.

By habit, she headed to the right toward her former office, realized her error, managed to angle her wings in the open atrium to the second floor and soared above the white marble floor inlaid with ruby. On the third level, four engineers rotated and spun three-dimensional gears and pulleys on a modern version of a Pegasus-drawn carriage. They waved at her, and she smiled and waved back. If she had a few minutes to stop, she'd love to see the eccentric cupids' new invention.

Instead, she entered her department, furled her wings, and gazed out the bay windows. The Fates River zigzagged toward Lake Aphrodite. What a view!

"Hey," her friend, Serenity, called.

Belle turned. Serenity tarried at a long white table next to the boss.

"We're revising your schedule," he said. The male, not much older than Serenity, wore a toga. Belle appreciated the casual atmosphere here, said to free creative vibes.

"You two have fun testing the holographic human this morning," he said.

"We will." As Serenity nonchalantly glanced over her shoulder, her strawberry blonde hair and fair skin made her seem innocent, while her long bob hairstyle framing her face made her look chic

"You dating him?" Belle asked, having witnessed a flicker of attraction in the boss' eyes.

"Not my type."

"If you say so." Later, Belle would grill her friend.

"We're in one of the experimental rooms on the third floor. Wait 'till you see the new prototype."

Belle didn't mind the break from analyzing and comparing the elements in love potion formulas. "What is it?'

"An interactive way to use the Book of Relationships. You know that book you used continually for the last two years to connect love."

"Don't remind me. I still have nightmares about manually

inputting the wrong data into the system and having unfulfilled soulmates chasing after me."

"If you changed them into soulmate Zombies, you'd have a blockbuster movie."

"You're too much." Belle shook her head.

"Is it possible that your previous assignment made you leery of falling in love?"

"I believe in love. Just not the forever kind of sappy love Cupids tout. And you're one to talk."

"I prefer playing the celestial field." Serenity snickered. "It's more exciting than being tied down to one guy."

Belle would probably feel the same if she were cute and spirited like her friend, not a tall, gangly misfit with dark auburn hair. "So how does the prototype work?"

"Our engineers transformed 2-D information into a human holograph. They think it will be a more exacting and exciting way to find matches. Having the information will better equip Cupids on their subject—love."

"Can't wait to see it. Studying humans and learning about their mannerism in a controlled environment makes sense." Belle followed her friend into Pod C, a space twice the size of her living room, and walked along the marble flooring on the right. Belle shivered.

"It is a bit chilly, but you'll get used to it."

In the center, a blue luminescent pathway formed. Inch-long squares embedded with an ever-changing series of molecular, atomic formulas. "Oh, my gosh, that's the basic structure of matter. I've always wanted to experiment with it."

"Watch this." Serenity reached down, carefully selected molecules from the floor, and held them in her hand. She used her fingers to create a glasswing butterfly. It flew around the room and landed on her finger.

"The butterfly looks real. Can I try?"

"Of course. Think about what you want to create. Once you have a clear vision of the molecular structure, go for it."

Belle concentrated, and a formula popped in her mind. She bent down and selected atoms in various sections of the changing floor. In her hand, she turned and twisted and watched molecular fusion in action. A red comb formed, followed by a beak, beady eyes, a white body, and feet. "I can't believe I made a chicken." She plopped the hen down on the floor next to her. It clucked, ran to her glittery shoes, and pecked. Its beak pinched her toes.

"Ouch! Knock that off." She stepped to the side, and the ridiculous chicken flapped its wings and followed her. "What should I do?"

"Break the code by setting your creation into the molecular floor." Serenity dropped the butterfly from her finger, and it dissolved.

Not about to touch her creation, Belle used magical dust from her fingertips to float the hen into the pathway. It disappeared.

"Why'd you pick a chicken?" Serenity asked.

"Meant to form a baby chick and messed up."

"And your grin says you had a blast. If you're ready to try out our simulated man, I'm gonna call C.I.P. to start the process." Serenity motioned to the see-through control panel along the wall.

Otherwise known as Cognitive Internal Processing, Belle was excited to see this virtual processor for the first time.

"Wake up, Cip," Serenity said.

A hologram man appeared. "Hello, Serenity. Who's your friend?"

"This is Belle Brooks."

"Very nice to meet you, Belle." His smooth, well-modulated voice reminded her of the local newscaster.

"Cip, please list four towns in Southern California that start with T," Serenity said.

"Temecula, Temple City, Tustin, Tranquility Village."

"Search Tranquility Village for men in need of a love match." Serenity's face lit with excitement as she tapped her foot and waited.

"I've located five-hundred matches. State a quality you're looking for."

"Belle, you pick."

Belle moved in closer. "List a man with a warm heart that needs mending."

"Thirty matches. To narrow your search, give a range in age."

This was fun. Belle chimed in, "Twenty-six to twenty-eight."

"Asher Killian O'Sullivan, who is nicknamed Lucky,

matches all criterion." The image of a dark-haired human with a day-old shadow on his chin appeared. "Shall I send Mr. O'Sullivan to the center of the blue pathway?"

"Yes, please." Excitement pulsed through her veins.

A man formed in the middle of the coded molecular lane.

"Not bad," Serenity said.

"He's amazing." Belle noticed how his leather jacket fit snuggly over his biceps. His faded jeans accentuated his tall, lanky build. The man triggered heat deep in her core. Crazy.

"Who are you?" He removed his sunglasses and suspiciously gazed at Belle, holding her captive, unable to breathe much less move.

"I'm Serenity. And this is my friend, Belle."

He glanced around the room and combed his hair back with his fingers. "Where in the hell am I?" This man wasn't real, but his disgruntled voice, wide stance, and folded arms reminded her of an Eros' male when provoked.

"Welcome to Cupid's Corner, Mr. Lucky O'Sullivan." Belle curtsied.

He glared. "You're aliens from Mars, right? Don't think I'll cooperate."

"We're not aliens." Serenity said.

"Let-let-let-let me-me-me-me-me." He stomped toward them and crumpled into the floor as his molecules dissolved.

The thought of losing the simulated man saddened Belle, which was silly. He wasn't even real.

"Friggin' Son of Zeus." Serenity cursed and covered her

mouth with her hand. “Obviously, the program needs some tweaking.”

“Are you all right, Serenity?” Cip asked.

“Yes, Cip. You may close down.” The interactive cognitive processor blended into the cloud-covered wall.

CHAPTER 2

Oh, joy. Weekly dinner at the family estate.

Belle's boyfriend, Wynton Aphrodite, parted the cloud doorway and ushered her inside the foyer with quartzite flooring embedded with bits of sapphires. "I'd love to live in a house like this." He said that every time they came here.

6:05 displayed on the ornate wall clock.

Late.

Based on her mother's scowl, offensively late.

Fashionably late, as far as Belle was concerned.

She entered the dining room and gave her mother the expected kiss on her cheek. "Hey, Mom."

"Glad you could make it," her mother nodded. To her left, Belle's grandmother, Grand Dame Maraschino Brooks, enthroned herself in a high-back chair with her stiff posture and perfectly coiffed hair. She didn't acknowledge Belle. Nothing new there. Belle had no idea why her mother never seemed to notice how Grand Dame snubbed her. Her mother didn't seem to mind being around Grand Dame. If Belle had a mother-in-law like that she'd stay far away.

Her grandfather smiled from the opposite end of the table from his wife.

Her family stationed themselves around the oval-shaped table etched with bows and arrows. Her mother's cherished crystal table—the table passed down for generations to the oldest daughter.

"Hi," her father said, and she hugged him.

"Hey, Cole." Wynton shook his hand. "Can't wait for another chess rematch."

"Me too." Her father eye's crinkled at the corner.

Belle and Wynton sat in the empty seats next to her mother. China and diamond-plated silverware adorned the table. She picked up her pink napkin embroidered with a bubbling brook.

Her father waved his hand and glasses of ambrosia floated down to the table. He toasted, "To eternal bliss."

Bliss. Belle would settle for more laughter.

"You're on, Pops." Her father motioned to his dad, her grandfather.

G-Dad winked at her as he stood. Ever since Belle was a little cherub, she had a unique connection with him. He spread his arms, showing off his white silk suit with a sparkly vest. "My signature dish for tonight is watercress and shallot soup." He twirled his fingers. A frothy white liquid filled their bowls with ribbons of vegetables. Brie, feta, and jack cheese kabobs with a flaming triangular-shape carrot tips sailed into the center.

"Bravo, Dad." Her Uncle Pete applauded.

Wynton devoured his soup. "Delicious, G-Dad."

Her grandfather grinned at his wife. Grand Dame must've hated his nickname because her cornflower blue eyes iced.

"We're ready for your flakey coconut biscuits," her father said to his mother, Grand Dame.

The persnickety woman produced a basket covered with a pink-and-white checkered cloth.

Belle stifled a laugh as she took one. The heavy biscuit could be used as an anchor.

Her Aunt Anita delivered simmering asparagus and mushrooms on tiny plates. Belle used her magic to design a platter with dragon fruit and kiwi. She floated the plate around for her family to add to their meal.

"Anything exciting happening at I.P.?" G-Dad said to Belle.

"Nothing I can discuss." She made a zipper across her lips.

"That's my girl." Her dad's encouragement warmed her heart with pride.

"Give a girl a bit of power and see how she gets." Uncle Pete teased.

Wynton's eyes glazed, clueless as usual. She'd dated him

for two years, on and off. Not the brightest star in the galaxy, at least he was dependable, plus her parents adored him. Wynton set his arm across the top of Belle's chair. It should have felt comforting; instead, it felt possessive.

"Still hard to believe Cami shot the wrong person. Heard she's finally fixed her mistake," her uncle said.

"It's been handled." Belle shrugged.

"Never cared for that girl. She's full of herself. Uppity because she won a couple of archery contests." Grand Dame sneered. "You never should have moved in with her."

No way was she going to mention that Cami recently snuck to Earth to be with her human lover.

"I like Cami," her mother said.

Belle gave her mom an appreciative grin.

Grand Dame raised a brow and glared at her mother. "Cami's engaged to Alexander Eros. I can't believe you've allowed that, Opal. You're well aware of how shady that Eros clan can be."

Belle glanced at G-Dad, knowing about the feud between the Brooks and Eros families. According to G-Dad, his grandfather Rufus was once the most influential and charismatic person in the town. Everyone looked to him for advice as he served as the council's chief board member. At the time, the Brooks family dominated the archery field. But one day, rumors about Rufus—spread by Arron Eros—claimed that his grandfather had an affair with a mortal. The Brooks family lost their position in society along with destroying their family's honor.

Since the day Rufus was voted out of the council, no Brooks' descendant had served on the board. With their status questioned, the confidence in their marksmanship slipped. And the Eros family eased right into their spot. G-Dad had said to have faith in an old legend. Supposedly, he'd heard that generations later, a Cupid relative would restore the family, although he wasn't exactly sure how.

"I've known Amos Eros since grade school and don't see a problem with him." Uncle Pete said, mostly to Grand Dame.

"I'd be wary. His brother, Andre, doesn't deserve to be the chief council member," Grand Dame huffed. She was working her way into one of her sour moods which rarely ended well.

"You're just sore because the council wouldn't approve that enormous bird sanctuary in the backyard.

"If Virgil served on the council, he would have approved it." Grand Dame folded her arms, let out a long sigh, and smiled at G-Dad. Crisis averted for now.

With the main course served and eaten, her father said, "Now for dessert." His reddish-gold magical dust swirled, and cherries jubilee floated in front of each person. Another flick of dust and a blue flame ignited on the top of the dish.

"Why does Cole always have to flambé his desserts?" Grand Dame whispered to Belle's mother. "It ruins the flavor."

"You don't have to eat it." Her mother sampled a spoonful. "Dear, this is superb." She turned to Belle's younger sister, Venecia. "I do hope you will play for us tonight?"

"It would be my pleasure." Venecia stood and gracefully walked to the harp near the window in the living room. With her hair coiled on top of her head, she held the sides of her long golden gown and eased into a chair. Her fingers glided along the strings as she played a classical tune.

As a little girl, Belle recalled waltzing in the ballroom with her dad to this tune.

"Why didn't you ever learn an instrument?" Wynton's voice ruined her reminiscing.

"I didn't inherit the gift." Envy for her sister crept inside Belle's mind and taunted her.

Her mom whispered to Grand Dame, "Venecia's harp instructor says she plays even better than Zinnia." A spoon fell from her mother's hand and clattered onto the table, and her hand covered her mouth.

"Who's Zinnia?" Belle's exceptional hearing homed in on the conversation, wondering why she'd never heard the name before.

Grand Dame's lips pursed; her eyes glinted daggers. "Don't talk about her."

What was up?

"Don't talk about who?" Uncle Pete asked as the song's tempo picked up.

"Zinnia." Belle's word floated out on its own accord.

"That name's never to be mentioned in my presence?" Grand Dame snarled.

"Why not?" her uncle asked. "She's your daughter."

"Not anymore. She's a disgrace."

"Because my little sister dared to defy you." Uncle Pete threw down his napkin and stood. "I'm out of here."

This was getting interesting. Belle glanced across at her grandfather. He sat ramrod straight. When his eyes caught hers, he quickly looked down.

"Belle," Wynton nudged her. "I have to get up at four a.m. tomorrow, so we'd better get going." He offered his hand.

Of all the nights to leave early, he had to pick tonight.

"I WISH you'd reconsider coming to Lover's Landing for this weekend," Wynton said as they flew along Bliss Avenue. He was running his aunt's watercraft business and wanted Belle to take tomorrow off and join him.

She'd opted out. Lately, she felt something was missing but just couldn't figure out what. "Long distance relationships never work."

"It doesn't have to stay that way. My Aunt April set me up with a houseboat right on the water. She wants me to relocate there permanently. If things go well, you could move in with me," he said as they landed at her apartment building.

"And leave the job that took me two years to get? No thanks."

"Then where does that leave us?" His shoulders sagged as he gave her a pained stare.

Her throat got dry. Wynton was nice. He came from the prestigious Aphrodite family which meant Belle could up her standings in society. Still, she didn't care about wealth. She didn't care about power. She didn't see a future with him. "We've had fun, but I think it's best we call it quits."

"You're breaking up with me?" His incredulous look said he was taken aback that she didn't jump at his offer.

"Think of it as allowing you to enjoy the next chapter of your life." She hoped her words would placate him. "I'm really happy for you. This is a great opportunity, one you'll excel at."

"You could always visit." His voice held a pleading tone. "Maybe during your next vacation?"

"I'd only distract you from your goals."

He kissed her cheek. "If you change your mind, the offer to move in with me will remain open."

She hugged him.

"I'll miss you, Belle." He held her for a while.

He wasn't a bad guy, just the wrong guy for her.

Parting the cloud-covered doorway, she lounged on a velvet chaise and wiped away a single tear. She'd been contemplating breaking it off with Wynton for a few weeks, but still, she doubted she'd ever find the right guy for her—especially in Cupid's Corner.

Maybe she should consider moving to another town. The added bonus—she wouldn't be required at her parents on Thursday nights.

Then she'd remembered the conversation about this Aunt Zinnia who was banished. What disgraceful act had she committed? Maybe she told Grand Dame off in public or ran away with someone below her station like a gardener or unicorn trainer. The mystery would drive Belle insane until she solved it.

A picture of Aunt Zinnia should be in one of her photo albums. Belle flicked her fingertips and swirled her silvery-violet dust. Even as a young girl, it bothered her that her mother and sisters had pink dust, not silvery purple like hers. She'd asked her father why she was different. He said to give thanks for the gifts the god of creation gave her.

She flipped to a photo of herself as a cherub clutching a stuffed unicorn. Underneath, she stared at her family's portrait. Her father held her ever-smiling older sister. Belle squirmed on her mother's lap.

She turned a few pages back to her mother's wedding. Wearing an off-the shoulders silk gown and a silver tiara holding her lacy veil in place, she posed for the camera. Her eyes radiated joy.

On the next page, Belle stared at the bridal party. Four groomsmen stood proudly on the left side, three bridesmaids were on the right with an obvious gap between the second and third Cupid. Another photo featured a family shot. Grand Dame and G-Dad posed to the left of her mother. Uncle Pete and her father had their arms around an empty space.

Besides being disowned, Zinnia's photos must have been expunged. Someone had tampered with the truth.

Why?

What could she have done? It had to be something horrible to erase all evidence of her existence.

She put the album away and called up her artificial intelligence assistant. "Hello, Claire."

A hologram, not much bigger than a glass of ambrosia, stood on the coffee table. "How may I assist you?

"Find Zinnia Brooks, please."

"Zero listings for Zinnia Brooks in this vicinity. Zinnia Zeus resides on Mount Olympus. Shall I connect you to her?"

"Claire STOP. DO NOT CONTACT HER." Belle's fear grew colder than the snow on the top of a mountainous peak. Cupids did not mix with the mighty Zeus family.

"Would you like me to check for Zinnia in other vicinities?"

"No, Claire." She shivered. What if her apartment wasn't a safe place to do research? To cover her tracks, she swirled her dust around the hologram. "Erase all previous searches and close down."

The image dissolved along with any record of Belle's search.

That was tense!

Still, nothing had been resolved.

How could she gleam info about her mysterious aunt? Uncle Pete might talk about Zinnia. Dratted Chaos, it was after nine And tomorrow morning, he and his wife were going to Mount Calypso for the week. Now what?

The cogs in her brain revolved faster than a merry-go-round on hyper speed.

She tapped her heart emblem and called her mom.

"Hey, honey. Is something wrong?"

"I can't stop thinking about Zinnia."

"We don't talk about her. Ever," she said quietly. "She doesn't exist for us."

"But—"

"I know how you hate to leave things alone, but this time let it go. And don't you dare bring her name up with anyone else." Her mother shut her down.

"Fine." Belle knew better than to argue with mom when she used that tone. "Good night."

If her own mother won't tell her, she highly doubted she'd get anyone else to talk. She'd have to figure this out on her own.

Where could she find unaltered information about her aunt?

The Cupid Archived Registry Database.

She had seen hard copies of the Cupid Registry Book for the twentieth century in the storage room at Cupid's Connections. She doubted anyone would even remember it existed.

Something about Aunt Zinnia should be listed there.

She crossed her wings for good measure.

CHAPTER 3

The following day, Belle's pulse quickened as she flew to the back section of Cupid Connection's basement. Two dozen labeled boxes lined the shelves. Birth records were on the bottom. She pulled out a book labeled 1900-2000 Cupid Registry and flicked her magical dust to send the registry to a desk drawer in her office upstairs. With that done, she slipped out of the room and flew above the stairs to the main floor.

The only sounds she heard were women chatting in the restroom, making it safe to flutter without notice through the atrium's center and up to the second floor.

"Hey, Belle." A younger male engineer called from over the railing on the third floor. "Got any plans for the four-day weekend?"

"Nothing definite yet. How 'bout you?"

"Got a gig playing harp at the jamboree in Lover's Landing."

The same town that Wynton headed to this morning. "Have fun." Belle ducked inside the Innovative Production's Center. The town's clock tower chimed eight times. An hour until she needed to clock into work. She veered into her office and retracted her wings. Easing into a cloud-soft chair, she gazed out the glass window that faced the I.P.'s main room. No one around. Good.

She opened the bottom drawer and floated the registry on top of her desk. To create a decoy while she searched the registry for Zinnia, she floated the Book of Relationships behind the registry.

Okay, what name should I open up in case someone comes in? That holograph guy, what was his name. Lucky. Lucky O'Sullivan. She typed it in. The pages flipped to Asher "Lucky" O'Sullivan. The two-dimensional photo failed to capture the virility she'd viewed in the life-sized holograph.

Forget the mortal and concentrate on the archive. "Find Zinnia Brooks," she whispered. The book's pages rifled to a Cupid. She scanned the information and rubbed her hands together. Her aunt's last residence—Friendly City, California.

The entry date was from twenty plus years ago. What had happened to her aunt since then?

She tapped her waist emblem and pulled up a virtual map of the area. Friendly City's south of Tranquilly Village.

Tranquility Village is Lucky O'Sullivan's hometown. What a strange coincidence.

She heard fluttering at the I.P. entrance and saw Serenity.

Keeping the Book of Relationships on her desk, Belle waved her hand, closed the page for the registry, sent it inside her bottom drawer, and added a locking spell. Determined to solve this mystery on her own, if she didn't find anything significant in the next week or two, she'd asked for Serenity's help.

Lucky O'Sullivan's photo showed from the open page on her desk. The handsome man's golden-brown eyes made her heart skitter.

Serenity came inside and stood behind Belle. "Was about to look up Lucky myself. We sure think alike."

"Wonder why they call him Lucky?"

"He's a hunk. Bet he has plenty of mortal women swooning." Serenity read the page. "Hmmm … it says his mother used to call him her lucky charm."

"Makes sense." A white light flashed on Belle's wrist emblem. "Got a message."

"So did I?" Serenity turned her wrist up. "Time for our department meeting."

Belle sucked in a deep breath. In her last department, meetings droned on for hours.

Serenity placed her hand on her shoulder. "The engineers are harmless but can get pretty intense."

"Is that why you never dated any of them?" Belle sent the Book of Relationships to its proper place on the bookshelf.

"Who said I haven't?"

They exited the office, entering the conference room. Seven engineers conversed around a long table closest to the bay windows.

Belle gazed out at the Fates River.

"Have a seat." Her boss, Skipper, said from the end chair. He motioned for Belle and Serenity to take the empty seats in the middle.

As Belle eased into her spot, she glanced around the table. Three women. Five men. Her tech classes in college had about the same ratio.

"Now that everyone's here let's get started." Skipper snapped his fingers, and a clear display floated above the center of the table. "Any problems with C.I.P.?"

"Cip's running well," Serenity said. "The computer interface's voice reminds me of a newscaster."

"He's come a long way. You should've seen Cip when he debuted five years ago. The machine malfunctioned hourly." Skipper hooked his thumbs underneath his red-and-white-striped suspenders. "On to our experimental prototype, Belle, please give us your unbiased opinion of the holographic human."

"It's quite impressive. Like an actual mortal stood in front of me."

"Were there any problems with the holograph?" a female engineer asked.

"The holograph operated perfectly at first," Serenity said.

"Then he seemed to sense he wasn't on Earth. It appeared as if we tapped into his inner self."

"Interesting concept. I asked the programmers for personality quirks, but I don't recall anything to do with self-concept." One of the engineers scratched his head. "I'll have to follow up on that."

"Please do. We'll invite the programmers to our next meeting. What happened next?" Skipper looked directly at Belle.

"A voice glitch occurred right after the subject, Lucky O'Sullivan, accused us of being aliens. He stuttered."

"And disappeared into the molecular field." Serenity cut in.

The engineers tossed out ideas about what might fix the malfunction and how to improve the holograph. Belle and Serenity added their input. Belle's mind filled with hypotheses. They discussed programming, computer glitches, and possible program design flaws. She adored being a part of this elite intellectual group.

"Since we're done here, and there's nothing pressing this afternoon, feel free to take off at two and start your Happy Hearts Holiday early," Skipper said as his lips curved into a smirk.

Everyone cheered. Whoever invented the holiday a hundred years ago was a saint. The idea—to restore energy drained by the hectic Valentine's season. The only agenda—relax.

"Get busy before I change my mind." Skipper smiled.

The others stood. Belle took a few steps.

"Belle, may I have a word with you?" Skipper asked in a businesslike tone.

She froze. Serenity mouthed, "Chill."

"Just wanted to say we're glad you're on our team." Skipper's warm eyes seemed sincere

Belle let out her breath. "I feel fortunate to be working here."

"You have a unique perspective. Since the prototype may not be ready to roll out for a while, you and Serenity will be studying our databases and checking for ways to make matchmaking more efficient. Serenity is already on board."

"So am I. Thank you for this assignment." She fluttered into her office.

AT PRECISELY TWO, Serenity and Belle zoomed out of the office building.

"Let's go to the spa?" Serenity asked.

"Not today. I plan on taking a long leisurely bubble bath." Belle flew next to her friend as they turned right on Bliss Avenue and parted the clouds to enter their apartment complex.

"First, share a bottle of ambrosia with me." Serenity stopped outside her ground floor residence.

"You're on." They entered the apartment. Belle sagged

into a fuzzy violet couch, admiring the lavender walls, plum carpet, and orchid inlaid coffee table.

Serenity popped a cork. Even the liquid she poured into two fluted glasses had a purple tinge.

Handing Belle a glass, Serenity moved on the couch beside her.

"I miss Cami." Her roommate had been gone for several weeks now, and the apartment seemed empty.

"Me, too. You've been friends for a long time."

"We met in grade school. Any word on her?"

"Not since she snuck back to Earth. She's in love. That's all that matters." Serenity gave a wistful sigh.

"How do you know this?"

"I saw her."

"What do you mean by *saw her?*" Belle was confused.

"I snuck down to check on her that first evening.

What the heck? "It's against Cupid Law to travel to Earth without permission."

"I'd do it again, but if I got caught, Cami's location might be jeopardized. We're the only Cupids who know she isn't in the Forest of Enchantment restoring her psyche," Serenity said quickly.

Belle's mouth dropped wide enough to catch a dragonfly. "Have you've been to Earth more than once?"

"Yes." Serenity didn't flinch as she held Belle's gaze.

"Wow. I'm impressed." If Serenity could do it, maybe Belle should venture down.

"I met Cami's human?" Serenity fanned her face with her

hand. "When I saw him kiss her, I could tell they would figure things out."

"Have you ever kissed a mortal?"

Serenity shrugged. "Nothing wrong with kissing."

"That's also against the rules." Belle's curiosity piqued. "Was it worth the risk?'

"Absolutely. Think about the thrill of racing a unicorn intensified a hundred times."

"That good, huh!"

"Sure is."

"I admire your bravado." She had to turn the conversation back to the technicalities of travel. "When you descended to Earth, did you take a sunbeam? It looked exciting watching Cami glide down."

"Once or twice. Sunbeam departures are monitored from nine to four. Sometimes a guard's schedule gets erased."

"By you?"

"Actually, I've never tried that." The grin that graced her face said she might in the future. "I usually travel by moonbeam."

"And how'd you figured that out?"

"From an encrypted message in an old book I found." Serenity smirked. "Moonbeams are similar to sunbeams."

"How are they different?"

"The strength varies according to the phases. What's with all the questions? You taking a trip?"

"Maybe someday." Like tomorrow.

"If I didn't already have plans for this weekend, I'd say

let's go tonight." Serenity finished her glass of ambrosia and used her magical dust to refill it. "More?"

"Please." Belle sipped her sweet drink. The alcohol made her bold. "Now you've got me intrigued. Explain the disparity in the moon's phases as it correlates with traveling."

"You're such a geek."

"And so are you. We're both pretty obsessed with scientific things."

"Yes, we are," Serenity said. "Traveling during a full moon is fairly straightforward. You pretty much land where you want. When you come back, the moonlight's power brings you to Cupid's Corner without notice."

"And if the moon is waxing or waning?" Belle needed every detail.

As the moonlight diminishes, so does your accuracy to pinpoint a destination. Once, I took a waning crescent down and ended up in San Diego instead of Los Angeles. Think it might've been fate intervening because I met a very entertaining sailor on leave."

"Of course you did." Her friend could be a little guy crazy. "What about coming back when the moon isn't full?"

"I've had to take a sunbeam at the first light to avoid the guards."

"Did you bring anything special with you?"

"Mortal clothing and money. Three hundred dollars seems sufficient, but I prefer to bring five or six." Serenity swirled her dust, and a bundle of bills landed in Belle's palm.

"What's this for?"

"In case you ever decide to sneak down. Twenties are the easiest to spend. I always keep money in my backpack just in case."

"Thanks. If I ever decide to go, I'll be prepared." Because of her friend's insights, Belle was now ready to find Aunt Zinnia.

"I'm all about being prepared." Serenity clinked glasses with Belle.

CHAPTER 4

Tranquility Village, California

Sixty degrees. Perfect weather for Lucky O'Sullivan to take his 1941 Knucklehead Harley on a brisk morning test drive. The cold air cleansed his mind. The sunshine brightened his mood. The motor's loud rumble invigorated his soul.

He stopped at a signal and waited to turn right. Five cars passed before he had an opening and rolled the throttle, only to have the engine sputter, spit, and stall.

His grandfather's words came back to him. "Give her a bit of sweet talk, and she'll usually cooperate."

He jumped off, pushed the motorcycle to the curb and put down the kickstand. The movement twinged the tendon below his kneecap.

He straddled the bike and stepped on the kicker. The engine coughed. "Guess your carburetor could use a little tweaking," he said to his Harley.

A motorcycle pulled up behind him and shut off the engine. His friend, Havoc, got off his Fat Boy Harley, a bike so new it still had temporary plates. "When you gonna get rid of this old relic?"

"Never. I happen to like vintage." Someday, he'd have his own shop.

Havoc took off his helmet and lowered his dark sunglasses "You gonna sit here all-day gabbing or do you need my help?"

Lucky kicked the starter one, two, three times. The motor engaged. "I'm good."

"Where you off to?" Havoc revved his engine.

"Gran's. She's making French Toast." He could almost taste the cinnamon flavoring in the sweet bread. His mouth watered.

"Think she'd mind if I tag along?"

"As if what Gran thought ever stopped you before." Lucky laughed. Havoc had invited himself over for meals countless times.

Rolling the throttle, Lucky revved the engine, popped the clutch, and rode off with his friend. The two of them roared past a strip mall. For the next three intersections, they sailed through green lights, made a right at the next street, and then a quick left.

Cruising under the jacaranda trees lining the block

toward a cul-de-sac, they slowed, climbing the cement driveway.

"Sweet gig you've got here," Havoc said as he got off his bike.

"Sure is." Living with his grandmother allowed him to put away money and keep an eye on the one person who'd always done her best for him.

It was home, sweet home.

Belle hadn't mentioned breaking up with Wynton to anyone, so her family should assume she spent the holiday with him. This worked to her advantage. No one would suspect that in a few hours, she'd arrive in California.

Still, breaking rules made her jittery. Visiting Earth without permission was a major violation but solving the mystery behind Zinnia trumped her usual wariness. She'd just have to be extra cautious. What could go wrong?

Plenty.

If she got caught, would the council banish her to a distant galaxy? She told her conscience to *shush*.

What to do first? Create a mortal outfit. Her favorite mortal actress was Emma Stone. Why not dress like her? "Claire, pull up photos of Emma Stone."

A thin screen floated in front of her with dozens of images. Sitting in a comfy chair, she used her finger to scroll through pictures. "I like that one." She tapped the actress in a bright yellow gown. The mustard color in the 3-D hologram would clash with Belle's complexion. Might as well keep searching. She paused at a lacy black dress. A bit too risqué.

Scanning through more images, she stopped at a scarlet-colored dress and stretched her fingers to make it full size. Spun the 3-D simulation to the side, then back. Cute with capped-sleeves and a skirt that flared, she figured the stretchy material would be comfortable. "Clare, create this outfit and include the denim jacket draped over the shoulder … and the shoes." The human style dress swirled around her body. Tall pointy pumps adorned her feet.

Perfect.

She wobbled across the room in skinny three-inch heels. On streaming television shows, mortal women didn't have any trouble strutting in these things. If they could do it, so would she. Walking to the living room and back to her bedroom, it took dozens of attempts to become steady.

She swirled her dust to remove her clothing and replaced it with a flowing white dress that touched the top of her knees. Her pink backpack with flashing white hearts lay on a shelf inside her bedroom closet. With another smidgeon of magical dust from her fingertips, she moved her backpack onto her bed and floated folded clothes inside. She added the packet of money from Serenity in a front pocket.

Her eyes drifted toward a shelf near the bottom of her bookcase where a keepsake box glittered with rubies and opals. She placed the box onto her bed, removed off the lid, pulled out a monographed handkerchief, her diary from grade school, a stuffed unicorn, the program from a ballet recital, a pink baby bonnet, half a dozen mathematical awards, a scroll with all her report cards, and an intricate interlocking cube. As a teen, she recalled frustration getting the quagmire puzzle to line up. But when she had, she found two glass bottles labeled invisibility potion.

How could she have forgotten about this? She and Cami sprayed each other. In seconds, they became invisible. Together they'd snuck in her dad's study while he and a colleague drank snifters of brandy and expounded useless banter.

Next, they had fluttered into her older sister's bedroom and read a page in her diary declaring her love for her newest beau. As the potion wore off, their bodies became transparent. They stashed the journal under the bed and ducked into Belle's room. Within minutes, they were back to normal.

Cami had said there must be a good reason for her to have such a powerful potion, insisting she saved the other vial for an emergency. Half the potion guaranteed Belle's getaway, the rest would allow her to remain unnoticed during her return.

She let out a relieved breath. Fate had given her a sign.

Now to remember how to undo the tricky puzzle. Closing her eyes, she visualized the sequence in her mind. Twisted the three sections to line up to the etching of an arrow. Pushed the center of the belly button on a cherub. A little door popped open, and a miniature skeleton key fell into her palm. Her hands shook as she inserted the key into a hole at the center. A quick turn and a silver chain with a tiny sprayer bottle dropped into her palm. The contents bubbled with a silvery-violet glow.

Yes!

She placed the necklace around her neck.

Amped about her success, she put her things away in the box, grabbed her backpack by a strap, went into the kitchen, and hung the flashing bag on the back of a chair.

Backpack, clothing, money. She made an invisible check with her finger.

Better eat something to give her energy.

Flicking dust, she conjured a croissant, two hard-boiled robin's eggs, and cut up dragon fruit. The sustenance should hold her through her uncertain night ahead.

Better pack snacks. She created a bag with mixed nuts and dried fruit, filled another with candy, grabbed two cherry-mango juice bottles from the counter, and placed the items inside her backpack.

Silver streaked through her violet colored wrist emblem. It seemed far too flashy for the human world. Tracing the heart with her fingertips, she used her magical dust, matching her emblem to her ivory skin tone.

I'm ready.

Glancing out the window, the moon wasn't visible.

"What time will the moon show?" she asked her virtual assistant.

"The waxing half moon will appear well after midnight."

She'd hoped for a full moon, but with the disappearing potion, everything should be fine. She waved her hand, told her virtual assistant to erase all search records, and repeated the process.

Since it was only eight-sixteen, she might as well take a nap. "Claire set my alarm to one a.m."

"Your alarm is set."

"Claire, please shut down."

She hung her backpack on a hook in her bedroom and settled under her comforter.

"WAKE UP, Belle, it's one a.m." Claire's voice said softly.

"One a.m.," she grumbled. "That came fast?" The lights on her backpack flickered. Securing the straps on her shoulders, she peered outside and pushed her window open less than a foot. A half-moon lit up the night sky. In theory, the beam should be fairly accurate to ride down.

Uncorking the potion, she sprayed herself. The contents smelled like molasses and ginger.

No turning back now.

The dust atomized. She stared down at her legs and watched them disappear along with part of her carpet. She could see inside the living room of the apartment directly below her, thankfully, empty.

No reflection showed from the mirror. Abnormal. Crazy. Spine tingling exciting.

In the blink of an eye, she flew south toward the Calypso Forest. A slight breeze pushed against her back urging her to hurry.

Flap. Flap. Flap. Wings fluttered past her, and she startled.

A speckled owl who-whoed.

Silly owl. Several yards further between two gigantic redwood trees, a moonbeam illuminated the area.

She slowed, glided to the edge, wrapped her arms around the luminescent column, and descended toward the Northern Hemisphere. Serenity said it may be necessary to manually manipulate the destination. Seeing the Midwest, she jumped onto a beam to the west and surfed it down toward Arizona. One more leap and she headed toward California. It appeared to be the southern part, although she wasn't certain where.

Thump.

She'd landed, straddling something hard. A streetlamp shone on a motorcycle. Easing her left leg over the side, she got off.

The bike wobbled.

"Please don't fall," she whispered.

It tilted to the left and crashed to the ground. Holy moly!

A man rushed to the front door of the building and yelled, "Lucky, your bike fell over."

She scrambled under the eaves, scooted against the brick wall, and lowered herself into a ball. Her fingertips brushed against her kneecap. She felt her thigh and her butt. Not only was she invisible but also naked and no longer Cupid-sized.

Why hadn't Serenity mentioned she might end up naked?

The door banged against a wall. A lanky man wearing blue jeans and a leather vest rushed toward his motorcycle and circled around it. "Shit," the guy's voice reverberated. "How the hell did it fall?" he asked the young couple standing along the curb.

"Beats me," the other man said.

"Might've been a Santa Ana gust," the woman next to him added.

The owner scowled and ran his hand along the gas tank, picked the motorcycle up, set the kickstand, and shook his head. "Looks like nothing's damaged."

"Must be why you're called Lucky," the woman simpered.

Lucky? Belle knew that name.

He turned and faced her. Dark hair, golden eyes. Simulation guy—in the flesh.

He walked with a slight limp inside the bar.

She traced her fingers along her waist. Still naked. Her throat narrowed. It became hard to suck in air. The potion would wear off in ten minutes or less. Good thing she'd packed that dress.

Taking the invisible backpack off her shoulders, she put it on the ground, unzipped it, and clutched the soft material. Without magical dust to fit clothing around her, dressing human style had better be easy. She managed to slip her right arm through one hole and her head through the other. The fabric trapped her left arm as she felt for the sleeve opening with her right. Where's the other hole? If only she could see the dress.

I have to fix this inside somewhere.

A man with embroidered wings on the back of his leather jacket pushed open the tavern door. She followed him, figuring anyone who wore wings should be all right. Now to find a private place at the back and fix her dress. The dimly lit room smelled like yeast, vinegar, and an unrecognizable odor. Her eyes adjusted to the darkness, and she peered into a full-length mirror a few feet from the bar.

No reflection of her yet. Good.

A scratchy unrecognizable tune drifted from the corner. She glanced around the saloon. A dozen people filled the round tables. Another dozen mortals loafed on bar stools or stood chatting in the aisle.

"It's quarter to two, folks. That means last call," Lucky said from behind the bar.

Several customers groaned.

That late already? Belle arrived at the moonbeam way after one and knocked down the motorcycle. Plus, fumbling with her dress took forever.

"I know. Time flies and all that." Lucky grinned. "Still, everyone leaves on the hour."

"Another draft," a burly man to her right called.

"Me, too," said the guy next to him.

Lucky tipped two clear mugs under a spigot, filled them with amber liquid, and set them in front of the customers.

Mesmerized by his succinct moves, someone's boot heels dug into her little toe. She bit her lip to keep from howling, hopped on one foot, and leaned against the polished bar.

"Sorry." A man stepped forward, turned his head, glanced around, and shrugged.

She waited several seconds for the throbbing to subside. A glimmer of her pink fingernail polish showed. Her pulse sped.

Get out of here.

A red exit sign flashed near the back. She ran toward the door with "Ladies" painted in black and turned the knob. Locked.

She scanned the area to see if anyone looked her way. Her hands and arms looked like tissue paper as she opened the last door on the left and stepped inside.

Unpacked boxes stacked five high on the floor on one side of the room. To her right vodka, bourbon, tequila, wine, pineapple juice, grenadine, and miscellaneous bottles were arranged in rows on metal shelving.

Her red dress got darker. No wonder this didn't work. She'd used the head hole for her arm and her armhole for her head. She pulled the dress off and adjusted it.

The rough flooring bothered her feet. Her dirty feet. She reached for her backpack.

Holy crap! She'd left it outside. Holy Zeus, she needed her bundle of money. She had to get out of here, pronto.

She twisted the doorknob and pulled. It wouldn't budge.

Panic shot through her system. Yanking with all her weight, she fell back into the wire shelf.

A beige bottle tumbled to the ground.

Cr-aaa-shhhh!

She somehow managed to scramble up. There has to be another way out.

The door slammed against the wall, missing her by two inches. "What are you doing here?" a man's voice roared. His eyes bored into her.

"Lucky?"

"Do I know you?" He raised a brow while folding his arms.

"Um, no."

"Who are you?"

"My name's Belle."

"Alright, Belle." He stepped closer, stood with his hips wide and intimidating. "You're paying for that broken bottle of Bailey's." He tapped his foot.

"I left my backpack out front. If you'd get it, I'll be happy to reimburse you." She hoped it didn't cost more than a hundred Earth dollars.

He glanced at her feet. "Right." His aura showed deep red anger. The fact that she could see it meant he must be livid.

"Believe me, it's out there."

"Of course, it is. I'll leave, and you'll help yourself to a couple of bottles on your way out."

"I'd never do such a dastardly deed."

"Wouldn't be the first time it happened." He swooped her up and held her over his shoulder.

"Put me down." Her feet dangled, and she kicked at him with all her might. "The broken bottle was an accident."

He opened the back door.

A cold breeze hit her face. She struggled to get out of his hold, and he lost his grip. The end result was an inelegant face plant against the asphalt. "Ouch."

"Are you okay?"

"As if you cared." She glared at him.

"I don't really. Anyway, show your face around here again, and you'll be arrested."

"You're a pompous jackass." She yelled as the door banged closed.

Her palms, elbows, and knees stung. Lucky O'Sullivan deserved to be thrown in Zeus' dungeon, taken as Poseidon's slave, or turned into a warty frog.

If only she had access to her magical dust.

Her palms throbbed from her landing on the hard asphalt. Gravel dug into her skin. She stood, brushed herself off, and glared at the backdoor of the bar where that cursed man treated her as if she were no better than rubbish.

In reality, Earth was nothing like the romantic movies she adored. What happened to the wondrous place full of friendly people?

Friendly. Not a word she'd consider to describe Lucky. Well, thinking about that horrible man would help her reach her goal. She'd risked plenty coming to Earth and wasn't leaving until she learned something about her aunt.

Sucking in a deep breath, she inhaled a foul odor from the boxy trash bin. Something buzzed past her ear. Was it a bee? Bees made honey. The tiniest smidgen made her break out in bumps, ugly itchy heartbumps.

She sprinted away from the trash bin, down the back alley of the bar, cut through an empty lot to the street, and spotted a sign near the front entrance.

Rebel Rouser Tavern.

The Dog House would be a better name. For hauling her outside, she'd love to see Lucky chained in front of a real doghouse.

Still, she needed the money inside her backpack to pay for a hotel. Stomping to the building's corner, she searched the ground. Lights from her backpack flashed against the brick wall. Thank you, Zeus.

Her knees ached as she reached down for her bag. Eyeing a bench across the dirt lot in front of Tranquility's Tattoos, she walked to it and plunked on the hard, wooden seat. Her bottom smarted.

Finding her backpack unzipped, she pulled out her shoes and let out a triumphant, "Yes!" She brushed off her feet and slipped on the tall pumps. Stretching her legs out straight, she flexed and pointed her toes. Nice.

Whump. The tavern door hit the wall, and people exited. A couple got into a pickup truck parked across the street.

Three men dashed into an old dented car. Folks started their motorcycles. Engines popped, and the bikes zoomed off.

The bar must've closed. What time was it anyway? She glanced at her wrist emblem and couldn't see it. Blending her wrist emblem to match her skin disabled her magical power. What an idiotic move.

A man on a motorcycle stopped near the curb and threw down a cigarette butt. "Need a ride?" He raised his visor, revealing shifty eyes and a nicotine-stained grin.

"No, thanks. Someone's picking me up."

"You're quite a looker. Come back to this bar tomorrow night, and I'll buy you a drink." He revved his engine and sped away.

Better hurry to that motel sign flashing to the north. She reached into her backpack for money. Where is it? She pulled out nuts, candy, and juice bottles. It has to be here!

Her stomach twisted.

Quit stressing. *I probably put it in the front pocket.* She unzipped it and felt inside.

No money.

She turned her bag upside down. A single red-hot candy fell out and hit the concrete.

It has to be here. She got up and searched the ground around the bench.

Nothing.

Think. Maybe it fell out as she headed over here, but deep in her psyche, she had her doubts.

She rose, wobbled to stay balanced in her stilted shoes, and stepped sideways.

Crrrrrrrraaack. Her heel broke, and she collapsed to the ground right into a mud puddle.

Damn heavy gravity.

She removed the other shoe and tried to break off the heel. It wouldn't budge.

Dumb, dumb, dumb trip to Earth.

I can't even go home because the moonbeam's light isn't strong enough, and sunbeams won't appear for hours.

"I hate this place." She slammed her heel on the ground. "I hate these shoes." She banged it. "Take that—you ridiculous high heel."

CHAPTER 5

Never in his life had Lucky scooped up a woman and lugged her out, but the word "scam" flashed across the stowaway's forehead. He refused to feel guilty about treating her no better than a common thief. Refused to think any more about that stranger.

He rushed inside behind the bar, ready for this night to end.

"What happened back there?" A sixtyish man, with a foot-long gray ponytail, asked.

Lucky wanted to snap, "None of your damn concern," but knew better than to piss off a cash-paying regular. He managed a disgruntled groan, and said, "Nothin'."

"Who's the gal you just carried out?" his friend, Havoc, asked. He swigged the rest of his beer.

"Don't know. Don't care." She had no business in the bar's

stockroom barefoot, wearing a red dress that melded to her body.

He had no business feeling a spark of attraction for her.

He glanced at the clock. Five minutes after two. Shit. That damn redhead ruined his concentration. "Bar's closed," he shouted louder than he'd intended. "Everybody beat it."

A scruffy man draped his arm around a petite blonde, and her high heels clicked across the room. A grizzly biker shuffled out behind a dozen other people.

Lucky approached a couple making out in the far back corner and cleared his throat. "Get a room."

The pair broke apart, and the man escorted his blushing buxom woman away.

Lucky locked the door and leaned against it. He'd lost his freaking focus because of one damn sneaky woman.

The blame game wouldn't get his tasks completed. He wiped down the counter. If only his grandfather were still alive. The old man's words echoed as clearly as if he stood right next to him. "Closing gives a man a chance to think."

Lucky never cared for quiet.

He brought three bags of trash out to the bin behind the bar and expected to see the redhead. Smart girl. She knew he'd follow through on his threat and call the cops.

Inside, he locked and bolted the back door. Then he double-checked the lock in front and brought the cash register drawer from behind the bar to his desk located on the far left of the storage room. He snagged a chair and counted a stack of ones, but soon lost track and rubbed his eyes.

Gotta focus.

Stretching his arms above his head, he cracked his knuckles and put his mind on his task. Entering the totals on the computer, he locked the cash inside a safe hidden behind a painting on the wall above him. Tomorrow morning, his business partner, Geezer, would take the money to the bank.

Done.

He glanced at the clock above the desk, figuring it'd be well past three.

2:49. Not bad.

I'll sleep well tonight.

His knee twinged. Not likely.

He grabbed his jacket and walked along the yellowed linoleum. Outside the entrance, he locked the deadbolt with a firm turn of the key.

Only one motorcycle remained out front. His Knucklehead Harley. The handlebars gleamed in the lamppost light. His engine fired up on the first kick. He eased out the clutch, moved forward, glanced across the empty lot, and spotted the redhead.

Dammit.

A MOTORCYCLE REVVED ITS ENGINE. It better not be cigarette man.

"Taking your frustrations out on a poor defenseless shoe." Someone said with a rip-roaring, aggravating laugh.

She looked up. Lucky took off his helmet and raked his fingers through his hair.

"You gonna call the cops on me?" She fisted her hands, ready to punch something or someone.

"For beating up a pair of high-heels. Nope," a chuckle stayed in his voice.

She wished this man would faint like a myotonic goat with a panic attack. At least that would take the smirk off his face.

"You okay?"

She hit the shoe again. "Just dandy. When I got to my backpack, someone stole my money."

"Sorry." He lifted a shoulder.

Temper flared through her veins. "What about calling the cops to find my money? You know the ones you threatened me with earlier."

"Believe me; it won't do any good when cash is missing." His jaw clenched, his eyes narrowed.

Somebody must've stolen from him in the past. Something big. Something he cherished. She sucked in a couple of deep breaths, and her ire cooled.

"Mind if I give that heel a whack."

"Have at it." Let him struggle as much as she had.

One hit, one tiny hit, and the heel flew off into the dirt lot. "Here you go."

She put the shoe on, not at all pleased with his success.

"Hey, it's late. Need a lift somewhere?"

"A hotel. You know any that will take pity on me and offer a room for free."

"I'm quite certain, they'll require a deposit. Given your history, well—"

"Do you have any other suggestions?" The hard bench wouldn't be a comfortable place to sleep. "Maybe a nearby park or something?"

"Hmm ..." He folded his arms. "I'm not sure the park would be safe, ... and ... by now, the closest shelter is probably full."

"Don't worry about it. I'm perfectly fine right here." She jiggled her foot. It'd be dawn soon, and she could go back to Cupid's Corner. No way. She came here to find her aunt.

"You can stay at my place." His dimples showed. He almost appeared trustworthy. Almost.

"That's okay." Knowing Mr. Throw-Me-Out-Like-Rubbish, he'd sacrifice her to a gryphon. She cringed. Her imagination went wacky when she was overly tired.

"Sleep in my studio apartment in the garage. My grandmother has a spare bedroom I can borrow."

"I don't get it. Less than an hour ago, you were throwing me out as if I were lower than pond algae. Now, you're nice. What's up?" She gazed at him, checking to see if he had horns.

"Guess I was a bit rough with you." He got off his bike.

"A bit."

"Did you skin your knees?" He stepped closer.

"Like it matters," she groaned. "You can leave, I'll be just fine."

"I can't leave you alone out here. It's not safe." He held up his hands.

"Why should I trust you?" She didn't get his considerate temperament.

"Because I have a sister about your age. I wouldn't want her out here alone. As I said, this area isn't safe at this hour for you."

Okay, he looked out for his sister. That didn't mean she trusted him, but a warm place to sleep did sound inviting. "It seems I don't have any other options." Her visit to Earth wasn't planned carefully. Now she had to accept this guy's supposed hospitality.

"You always this obstinate?" he asked, with a beaming smile.

"You always this contrary?" She couldn't resist bantering back.

"Yep." He placed his helmet on her head and adjusted the strap under her chin.

She looked up and met his eyes. Her heart thumped hard against her chest.

No, it didn't.

He slid forward. "Hop on, and we'll get going."

She eyed the seat. "I'm not sure what to do."

"Step on the peg and swing your leg over."

A bit awkward in a dress, she climbed on.

"Put your arms around my waist and hold on tight." The Harley accelerated forward, and the front lifted.

Her breath hitched as the wheel lowered.

"You okay?"

"Fine." She grasped his body as they rode up the street. The cool night air hitting her face reminded her of flying.

He waited for a car and turned left. They passed Tranquility Village Community Center, made another left, a quick right and putted under a canopy of trees.

With the help of street lamps, Belle admired the cottages and homes lining both sides of the street. "Charming neighborhood."

"Never paid it much mind," he slowed at the cul-de-sac, rode up a driveway, and clicked off the motor. "The garage is separate and behind the fence. Think you could get off and open the gate, so I can walk my bike to the back."

"Thought you lived in a studio?" she asked as she pulled up the latch and eased the gate forward.

"It's an add-on to the garage." He pulled up a large wooden door and wheeled the motorcycle inside.

"Oh. So that's your grandmother's house." She pointed to the pink, one-story, stuccoed home.

He nodded and gave her a don't-even-think-about-asking-more look. Probably embarrassed, but he shouldn't be. He had his own space.

"You bring any other clothes besides that ratty dress." He kicked a plastic bag filled with clothing.

"I'll have you know, this is a designer gown." Designed by her with magic. "At least it was until—"

"I threw you out. I get it. But I didn't sink you into that mud hole. That you can blame on those." He pointed to her shoes.

Too tired to come up with a sarcastic retort, she tapped her foot.

"I just changed the sheets on my bed and don't want mud on my pillow. You're in luck; my sister's discarded clothes didn't make it to the Salvation Army."

She glanced at her ripped and soiled dress. "I'm not changing here."

He let out an annoying howl. "Didn't ask you to, princess."

Princess? The term curdled her stomach. He hefted the large sack as if it weighed less than a feather. She ignored how the muscles on his arms rippled, ignored how his Levi's accentuated his firm buttocks, ignored that her eyes found him hot. What did her eyes know anyway?

"You coming'?" Did his mouth have to quirk up as she handed him the helmet? Annoying. He ushered her outside, shut the garage door with one hand, and led her to a rectangular add-on to the right. "Here you go." He turned a knob.

She expected to see clothes on the floor, maybe motorcycle parts scattered on the table, a bed unmade, but not a tidy room.

He set the bulk of clothing on the floor. "The bathroom is

at the back. Feel free to use the shower. Clean towels are on the rack, extras in the cabinet. Shampoo and everything's on a shelf inside. If you can't find pj's in that bag, feel free to borrow one of my T-shirts in the closet."

The thought of his shirt against her body made her face get hot. Weird reaction for a human she barely knew.

"Thank you." What's up with his niceness? Her brain hurt trying to figure out this enigma of a man.

"The coffeemaker's set to go off at eight. Cups are in the cupboard above the sink. Help yourself to any food in the fridge but not in the freezer." He motioned to a white box on the counter not much bigger than three or four loaves of bread.

"Why not?"

"Because I said so." His eyes twinkled.

"You're teasing me."

"Nope. Sleep well," he said, his voice deep and sensuous. The dratted man whistled as he walked out.

She tried to pick up the bag with one hand, and a piece of plastic tore off. Using both hands, she poured the items on top of the patchwork quilt covering the massive bed that took up half of the room. She imagined him lying on his back, hands above his head, gazing at her with hooded eyes.

Don't go there.

She picked up a pair of silky pajamas. Cute.

Now for that shower. Her knee smarted from falling earlier.

The bathroom wasn't spacious, but it was clean. Glancing

in the mirror, she had a large smudge of mud caked on her chin, and more mud-streaked through her wild, curly hair. No wonder he'd laughed at her.

She pulled off her dirty dress, dropped it on the pristine black and white checkered floor, opened the clear glass door of the corner shower, and climbed inside. She waved her hand to turn it on. Nothing happened.

Right. This wasn't home.

She pulled out a knob and water hit her face. Cold water covered her. Every scrape and scratch burned. Aching and shivering, she needed to get rid of the mud and dirt and stayed under the spray. Turning the knob to the left, the water warmed. "That's more like it."

The shampoo on the shelf belonged to Lucky. She poured a glob into her hand expecting an earthy, not lemony scent. Lathering her hair, the shampoo smelled better than her favorite cherry vanilla. Water cascaded down her shoulders as she rinsed.

The pine scented soap seemed to fit him. As she used the bar, she tried not to think of him rubbing this same bar along his chest, stomach, and—

She turned off the water, stepped out, and wrapped a soft towel around her body. That shower soothed her muscles. Her knees still hurt, but not as bad. She slipped the pajama top over her head and weaved in her arms. For the bottoms, she stood on one leg and managed to get the right one inside, shifted her weight and managed to pull up the other leg. Dressing without magic sure was exhausting.

Wide-awake for such a late hour, she sifted through the clothing. A beige sweater came to her knees. She brought a pair of jeans against her. A little short, they should fit. She grabbed some maroon colored Bermuda shorts as back up, added a green blouse, hooded sweatshirt, and a stretchy white bra for tomorrow. She found underwear still with a price tag of ten dollars. It's bad enough to be wearing hand-me-downs, but she drew the line at underwear. She'd rather go commando than do that.

She stacked the clothing on the dresser, and a big yawn escaped. Debating over black boots or sneakers, she placed both of them on the floor and shoved the rest of the clothing back into the bag.

"Don't look in the freezer." Why'd he say that? She had to look. What if there's a human head inside like in a scary movie? Go to bed. Forget about looking.

Her curiosity got the better of her.

Tiptoeing, she opened the refrigerator door. Energy drinks. A dozen power bars. A six-pack of beer. A carton of eggs.

Now for the freezer.

Don't be a body part. Don't be a body part. Don't be a body part.

Slowly, she pulled on the handle. A package of Chocolate Ganache ice cream cones. Really?

Again, she yawned. She settled into the bed and breathed in the woodsy, lemony scent on his pillow—like Lucky, sinful and fresh.

CHAPTER 6

Bark. Bark, bark.

The dumbass neighbor's dog ruined Lucky's sleep. He peeled his eyes open to hideous rose, tulip, and daisy wallpaper. Why was he in Gran's flower land bedroom?

Because that attractive, clueless redhead slept in his bed. He glanced down at the pansy bedspread and wanted to gag. Even the musty air smelled of potpourri.

7:06 a.m. flashed from the nightstand clock.

Lucky didn't get to bed until well after three. Most of the night, he'd tossed and turned thinking about that woman. He tried not to imagine her violet eyes that drew him in. He tried not to imagine her short dress that accentuated her gorgeous legs.

She seemed sweet, although a bit off. He felt terrible she'd lost her money, however leaving her backpack outside was an airhead move. And why was she barefoot in his stockroom?

Too early to be this wide awake, he booked for the kitchen to grab a cup of coffee.

A little caffeine and he might be ready to check on the visitor in his room. If he were blessed, she would have already split. Not likely.

Gran loitered at the table.

"Isn't it a little early to be playing Bubble Gum?" His grandmother had become addicted to this useless phone game.

"It's Bubble Witch. Just earned five hundred points in the last ten minutes."

He groaned.

"Something wrong with your room?" More ridiculous popping came from her cell.

"Nope."

"Spill," she said as he strode past her. A car honked, and she stood. "You're off the hook for now 'cause Gladys is picking me up for yoga. When I get back, I'll expect answers."

The door slammed, he let out a deep breath and filled his coffee cup. Gran had the habit of rescuing strays and finding the perfect home for them. If she met the woman, his grandmother might think of her as a lost puppy or kitten. He barely knew the woman and planned to drop her at the bus depot where he'd buy her a one-way ticket home.

He grabbed a bagel from a bag on the counter and bit into it. Stale, he dipped it in his coffee and had another bite.

Disgusting. Dropping the bread into the trash, he gulped the rest of his coffee, marched to his place, and knocked.

She answered the door wearing silky pajamas. Her mussed hair gave him the impression she'd tossed and turned during the night.

"Mornin', princess. Get dressed. I'm dropping you off at the bus stop." The sooner she was gone, the happier he'd be.

She blinked several times and stared at him. "Good morning."

"We need to get going." He had to get her out of here before Gran or his nosey sister saw her. Knowing either one of them, they'd invite her to stay indefinitely. "If you hurry, I'll take you to breakfast?"

The side of her mouth lifted. "I'd like that."

She might be pretty but was also either clueless or crazy. Maybe both.

THIRTY MINUTES LATER, Lucky and Belle waited in a booth at Rover's Diner. Belle sipped tea. He drank black coffee.

"Since I was kind enough to offer you my bed last night, well—" He cleared his throat. "Wanna tell me what you were doing at my bar?"

"I came to visit my aunt." She fiddled with her napkin.

"You thought you'd find her inside?" Her aunt might be a lush, and Belle planned to take her home. He'd seen that scenario plenty of times before.

"Not exactly."

He silently counted to ten. Apparently getting a straight answer out of her would require a keg full of his patience. "You were saying you came here to visit your aunt and got sidetracked." If she wouldn't tell her story, he'd make one up for her.

"I took the … bus … and planned to get off in Friendly City. Somehow, I got mixed up." She blushed. Her rosy cheeks made her even prettier.

"You got off at the wrong station?"

"Um … yes," her voice hitched. "And I got lost. Before I spotted the sign for … your tavern, my feet were killing me. So I removed my shoes." She looked away.

As a bartender, he'd learned to read people. What wasn't she telling him? "At least that explains why you were barefoot.

"Ready to order?" a middle-aged waitress asked.

"I'll take blueberry crepes with extra whipped cream and walnuts sprinkled on top."

Bold for someone who was penniless, he kinda liked Belle's grit.

He ordered the lumberjack breakfast, and the server scurried off.

"Okay, you got off at the wrong station, but my place is over a mile away, and it was late. Didn't you expect your aunt or someone else to pick you up?"

"No." She focused on the wall behind him. "I just learned my dad has a sister, a sister nobody ever talks about. Her name slipped out a couple of nights ago during dinner at my parent's house."

"So, you decided to find her."

"I planned to stay in a motel overnight, assuming I'd connect with Aunt Zinnia in the morning." Uncertainty flashed in her eyes.

The waitress brought their food. Belle took a bite of her crepe. "This is delicious." She ran her tongue along her lips, and his lower extremities twitched.

He polished off three strips of bacon.

"Is Friendly City far?"

"About an hour as long as traffic's light. You know her address?"

"Bright Street." She looked up as if the answers were on the ceiling. "808 … Bright Street."

She had a logical reason for being here. His shift didn't start until six, and he wouldn't mind a long ride. "I can take you there if you'd like."

Once he dropped her off with relatives, he'd come home and get some sleep.

But could he survive nearly an hour with her arms wrapped around his waist, her body pressed against his back?

Offering his assistance hadn't been very astute.

My gosh, Belle liked riding on the back of Lucky's Harley. The machine growled beneath her. She clung tight to him as they rode along a tree-lined boulevard. The scent of oil and exhaust excited her, or maybe it was the mortal.

He could've dumped her off at the nearest bus station; instead, he offered to bring her to her aunt's city. The fact he rode a Harley—an added bonus. Wearing a leather jacket, for today he could be her rebel fantasy.

They passed dozens of three-story apartments. A cluster of women pushed strollers. On the sidewalk, a man ran with his dog.

"You okay going fast around curves?" he shouted.

"Sure. The faster the better." Adrenaline thrummed through her body.

"You're my kind of girl." His throaty whisper caused a shiver of desire. "Remember to lean with me when we turn."

As she pressed against Lucky on a vehicle close to the ground, they weaved along the winding road.

"Steep embankment to your right."

She cinched her hold around his abs, trying to concentrate on the road and not his muscular body. To her right, the shoulder dropped off for miles, but she wasn't worried. Not with the way Lucky maneuvered this bike.

They reached the elevation marker of 3000 feet. The condensed houses spread out. Scattered homes and ranches dotted the grassy landscape. Livestock grazed. The setting reminded her of a picturesque country painting.

They continued and eventually forked left onto a two-lane highway. Gravel crackled under the tires as they reached the summit sign: Friendly City, Population 10,750.

If things went well, soon she'd meet the banished Aunt Zinnia. Would she be receptive or blow her off? She swallowed, her mouth dry.

"The town's right over the ridge," Lucky called out.

The road dipped, and her chest thudded against his back. "Sorry."

"You don't sound the least bit sorry," he said with a low tone.

She wasn't.

CHAPTER 7

In a few more minutes, Lucky would drop off the pretty redhead. He should be relieved, but to be honest, he liked having her on his Harley. They came to the center of town, passing housing tracts, liquor stores, smoke shops, gas stations, and the Tipsy Cow Bar.

Lucky turned on Bright Street, slowed, and checked the numbers painted on the curb. "You did say 808?" He pulled in front of a purple bungalow.

"Yes." As she got off, he tried not to focus on how those jeans hugged her butt.

She pivoted, her rounded eyes reminding him of a lost kitten. "You're coming with me, right?" Her voice sounded soft and cautious.

"If that's what you want."

She stumbled on the cracked sidewalk.

"Careful." He caught her by the back of her arms and steadied her. The simple touch had him longing to turn her around and press his lips against hers. In a different situation, he might act on his impulse. Not here.

They walked up the steps together. A porch swing hung by rusty chains. Her body stiffened as she tentatively knocked on the front door.

"Relax. You'll be fine." He pretended to predict the outcome.

Belle gave him a guarded smile.

The door opened to a six-foot, big-boned, buxom woman with a black Liza Minnelli style wig. "Hello," she said with a baritone voice, batting her eyelashes and showing off turquoise eye shadow.

"Aunt Zinnia?" Belle asked.

As a bartender, he'd seen just about everything. Thus, the matter didn't surprise him.

"No one here by that name, honey. My stage name is Lady Lavender, but you can call me Paul." He put a hand on his hip.

"Well, Paul, my aunt lived here about twenty-five years ago. You wouldn't happen to know where she went?"

"Only been here about six months. You should try Mildred's across from the Lazy Eight Motel on Main Street. She seems to know everyone in town." A smudge of red marred his front teeth. "Hope you find her. Bye-bye." He gave a funny wave and closed the door.

"That didn't go like I expected." In his experience, things rarely did.

"I was so certain I'd meet my aunt today." Tears filled Belle's eyes as she moved toward his bike "Would you mind taking me to that woman's shop?"

He'd already come this far and couldn't leave with good conscience and not follow through. Besides, his curiosity had been piqued. "No problem. But then I'd better head back. After I drop you at the bus station in town, I need some sleep before my shift tonight."

He glanced toward the house. The curtain pulled back from the window, and Paul peered out. "You know, one Halloween I dressed up as Marilyn Monroe." He straddled his Harley.

"Did you shave your legs?" She giggled.

Good. He made her laugh. "You've got to be kidding. If the bikers in my bar got wind of a crazy stunt like that, I'd never live it down."

Five minutes later, Lucky waited with Belle outside a green building with Mildred's Boutique on a wooden sign.

He checked his cell. "It's close to ten-thirty. Shop should've opened at ten." If he were this late at his saloon, his regulars would complain.

"Give her five more minutes, please." She shifted back and forth on her feet.

"Okay."

An old Cadillac rattled into a parking space. The door creaked, and a tiny woman with clunky shoes stepped out.

She wore a red silk dress with a matching boa. "Hope you haven't waited long. Got on the phone with my sister and woo-ee that girl blathers on." Her hands shook as she fumbled with her keys.

"May I give you a hand?" he offered.

"That would be wonderful."

He clicked the lock and held the door for the women.

The owner winked at Belle. "Men with manners don't come along very often. This one's a keeper." The woman turned around the sign and opened the blinds.

Inside the shop, straw hats and a spectrum of feathery boas lay strewn above a rack filled with dresses and skirts.

Mildred fiddled with the register.

A cuckoo clock sounded from the wall. Half a dozen other clocks chimed at different intervals. How annoying. "Belle, tell the lady why we're here."

"I'm looking for my Aunt Zinnia."

"Zinnia, hmm ... sounds familiar."

"Her maiden name is Brooks. She supposedly lived in this town about twenty-five years ago."

"Zinnia Brooks. I'm pretty sure she hung out with my great niece."

"Think you could call her and see what she remembers?" Lucky's knee stiffened, and he rubbed it.

"Would but she's out of town and won't be back 'till late tomorrow night." The owner turned to Belle. "Give me your number, and I'll have her call you."

"I forgot my phone," she said in a small voice.

He hardly knew her. The smart thing to do would be to wash his hands of her, but she needed to know the truth and dropping her off now would be heartless. And to be honest, he was curious. He handed the woman his business card. "Then call me."

Shit. This meant Belle would be with him for another night, and he'd have to explain staying in Gran's guest room. He snatched a fuchsia boa from the rack for a gift. "And ring this up for my grandmother." The vibrant color suited her eccentric style.

BELLE WATCHED Lucky place the feathery scarf in a saddlebag attached to the back of the seat. He'd bought a boa for his grandmother. It was rather sweet. He obviously cared a great deal for her. This compassionate guy was a far cry from the unyielding man she'd first encountered.

"Okay, I'll admit it. I have a thing for feathers."

"I get fetishes, but that fuchsia color washes out your skin tone."

He laughed a wondrous, full-on laugh. "What do you suggest?"

"Stick with earth tones that bring out the golden flecks in your eyes."

"You're pretty brazen considering I'm you're ride." He straddled his motorcycle.

"Sorry." Would he leave her here?

"Don't be. I like it when you're sassy."

"Yes, sir." She saluted him.

"Hop on, princess."

"You taking me to the bus station?"

"If that's what you want."

Maybe he'd let her stay another night? She eased behind him. "I'd rather stick around until tomorrow and hear what Mildred's niece has to say about my aunt."

"Well, what's in it for me?"

"I'm willing to negotiate."

"Let me think on it." He put the bike in gear.

What would he come up with? Serenity's talk about kissing a human had her considering the idea. Since he hadn't made a pass at her yet, what made her think Lucky might be interested in her that way.

Besides, she didn't need to be lip-locking with him. Her only purpose for this visit was to find her aunt. Period.

Holding her arms around Lucky's waist, she could feel his abs tighten. What would it be like to have him press her against the wall as his mouth descended on hers?

Ignore the absurd notion.

She glanced at strip malls and gas stations. They turned onto the highway toward Tranquility.

"What's with the silent act?" Lucky asked.

"Just pondering."

"Who says pondering these days?" he chuckled.

"I do. What's wrong with that?"

"Nothing, if you're my grandmother's age." He sounded far too resolute.

"I'll have you know, pondering is one of my favorite things to do."

"Don't worry about our negotiation. I've already thought up a few interesting propositions."

"Propositions such as?"

"You'll find out soon enough."

She didn't respond, opting to be quiet.

"We're coming up on the windy part. I'll be leaning left around the next corner."

They reached the city limits for Tranquility. "Since you'll be spending another night in my room, I've come up with an idea that might benefit us both."

She loosened her arms.

"I wasn't talking about sleeping arrangements." He turned left. "You could mop the stockroom in my bar."

She had never done chores without magic but would be willing to try. "I thought you'd call the cops if I came inside."

"That was before I knew you."

"You trust me now?" She found that hard to believe.

"Pretty much." He pulled up the drive. "If you're good, I may have you tally our inventory."

"Isn't that like allowing the fox to live in the henhouse?"

"You're funny."

She got off the bike and opened the gate.

"Ready to meet my family."

Family, as in a mortal family. "Not really."

"At least you're honest," he said.

If she were honest, she'd tell him she was a Cupid. That wasn't going to happen ever.

CHAPTER 8

Lucky pulled into the driveway behind Gran's old Buick.

"What time is it?" Belle asked.

"About noon." He clicked off his engine. It clunked. Clinked. Coughed. And died. "You've gotta love the quirks of a V-twin engine."

"What's a V-twin?"

"A two-cylinder, forty-five-degree, pushrod overhead."

"You mean it has two valves. I'd love to see how it works." Her face flushed talking about an engine. Impressive.

"Another day." If he started talking about Harleys, he could go on for hours. He brought his bike into the garage. "Have a seat at the table, and I'll find us something cold to drink." He pointed to four white chairs on the patio, opened the back door, and called inside. "Gran, I'm home."

"Over here." She reclined on the sofa with her phone in hand.

"I've brought a friend with me." Lucky shielded his eyes against Gran's neon yellow top. He smiled to himself. At seventy-years-old, she could get away with flamboyant colors.

"Is that the reason you slept in the guest room?" she said.

"Yep."

"What's she like?"

"What makes you think my friend's a woman?"

"Because I peeked out the window when you pulled up." Gran gave him a sideways glance. "Just whipped up a fresh pitcher of lemonade. You mind if I bring some out to her?"

"Sounds delicious." He kissed the cheek of the woman who'd always been there for him. "You're the best," he said and proceeded outside.

Pausing on the bottom step, he watched Belle examine a circular feeder under the eaves of the house. Year after year, the hummingbirds came back to feed on the honeysuckle flowers. The sight of the birds brought back memories of the first time he'd helped gran mix sugar and water and fill the bottle. Those were simpler times.

A purple hummingbird landed on a perch.

"Hey."

Belle startled. Her violet eyes were about the same color as a hummingbird's wings.

Gran walked out holding a pitcher in one hand and three

stacked glasses in the other. "In case you haven't guessed, I'm Lucky's grandmother."

"This is Belle." He passed out Gran's pink flamingo embellished tumblers and poured the icy liquid.

"Hello," Belle said softly.

Gran lowered herself and quickly scooted her chair inches from Belle. "What brings you to Tranquility?" She twirled a strand of her gray hair with purple streaks.

"Actually, I was supposed to go to Friendly City, but somehow got off at the wrong stop."

"And wandered into my bar last night," Lucky added.

"How interesting." Gran had a knowing gleam. He wasn't sure what that meant.

"I'm looking for my aunt. I just learned about her last week." Belle rubbed the back of her neck.

"Do tell." Gran raised a brow. "I do adore a good mystery."

"At our family dinner, I overheard my mother mention Zinnia's name. Apparently, she's my aunt. When I asked about her, everyone got quiet." Belle's lips pressed together.

"Bet she married the wrong person. My parents forbid me from seeing an Irishman but couldn't stop us from eloping."

Lucky heard this story before but didn't mind hearing it again.

"I offered to take Belle to find her aunt." He left off the part where he kicked her out of his bar. It gnawed at his conscience to not be forthright. "That's where we went this morning."

"But Aunt Zinnia doesn't live there anymore." Belle glanced his way.

He cut in. "Might have a lead. Won't hear anything until Sunday evening."

Gran's expression softened. "So you're staying another night?"

"If it's not too much trouble."

"Not at all. What's your aunt's full name? I might recognize it."

"Zinnia Brooks."

"Doesn't sound familiar." Gran folded her hands.

A hummingbird zipped over and sipped nectar at a feeder under the house's eaves. Belle gazed at it.

"That's a violetear. Its green wings glimmer like emeralds." Gran gave a dramatic sigh. "Keep watching the feeder. We might catch a ruby-throated hermit or black-chinned variety."

"That'd be nice." Belle's expression turned serious. "Hope you don't mind that I borrowed clean clothes from that bag?"

"What bag?" Gran eyed Lucky.

"The stuff sis left in the garage. Belle lost her luggage."

"Thought those jeans looked familiar." His grandmother chuckled. "Help yourself to whatever's out there."

He yawned. Tossing and turning in Gran's uncomfortable twin bed in the guest room left him tired. "Belle, we're heading for Rebel's around five-thirty. Plenty of time to catch some sleep and get ready."

"A nap sounds delightful."

"Go on," Gran said.

Belle traipsed toward his room. The subtle sway of her hips forced him to swallow a groan.

"What made you help that girl?" Gran arched her brow.

"I didn't at first. In fact, I found her in the stockroom next to a broken bottle of Bailey's and kicked her out."

"Makes sense." She rested her elbow on the table.

"At the moment, it did. But later after the bar closed, I found her outside, alone, and penniless because someone stole money out of her backpack."

"You played the hero and gave up your room?"

He was no hero. "I thought what if this were sis out there? Anyway, I'm gonna get some shuteye."

BELLE WOKE from her nap refreshed. She shuffled through the plastic bag on the floor and pulled out a lacy blouse. Long-sleeved, it tapered in at the waist and flared out with a scalloped hem. Might be dressy for mopping and inventory, but she tried it on anyway. Cute. She grabbed a pair of jeans, held them against her. A bit short. They should work.

Brushing her hair, she thought about Lucky. Unlike most Cupid men, he listened and acted as if her opinions mattered.

It was nearly five, giving her thirty minutes before she and Lucky would leave. She used the door on the outside wall and went into the backyard. Gran watered flowers and waved.

"Need any help?"

"Just finished." Gran turned off the spigot. "Come inside so I can introduce you to Lucky's sister."

"Sure." She followed Gran into the living room.

A chestnut-haired woman lounged on the couch with her legs on the coffee table. "Hi."

"Farryn, this is Lucky's friend, Belle."

"Nice to meet you." She tilted her head and stared at Belle. Her light brown eyes and fair complexion resembled Lucky's. "Gran says you'll be staying the night."

"I am. I'll be helping Lucky at the bar tonight."

The sister squinted. "Is that my blouse?"

"Was." Gran eased onto the couch and motioned for Belle to take the spot next to her. "She lost her luggage and borrowed from the donation bag."

"Then I'm glad my clothes went to good use."

"Heard Lucky took you to Friendly City on the back of his Harley?" She scrunched her nose. "You're one brave lady."

"I found the ride invigorating."

Farryn snickered. "Where you from?"

"Heavenly Valley."

"Love that place. You ski or snowboard?"

"Snowboard."

"Me too. Killebrew Canyon has some gnarly cliffs and chutes."

Belle nodded, pretending she'd been there.

"Okay, now for the million-dollar question." His sister eyed her with an inquisitive tilt of her head. "Saw Lucky on the bed in the spare room with his feet dangling off the end. How'd you get him to give up his place?"

Belle just smiled.

The doorbell rang.

"Pizza's here." Farryn hopped up.

"Lucky walked in combing his wet hair. "Hope you ordered my half with mozzarella and anchovies."

My gosh, he was hot.

"Of course and the other half's veggie. That okay with you?" Gran asked Belle.

"It is." Belle followed the group into the dining room and sat to the left of Lucky.

"Belle, you want one of each?" Lucky asked as he lifted the box's lid. His knee tapped her leg. A jolt of heat sizzled where it hit.

"Just veggie," her voice cracked. She bit into it and licked her lips. "This is really good."

"Take a taste of mine. It's way better."

"Not with that shiny little fish on top."

"Looks like I'm not the only one with good taste." Farryn high-fived Belle.

"It's acquired." He grinned. His dimples showed, making him oh so handsome. "Next time, I'll get pepperoni, just for you sis."

"I doubt that." Love shown in his sister's eyes.

For some odd reason, Belle felt more at ease around this family than she ever had with her own.

CHAPTER 9

Rebel Rouser Tavern, 9 p.m.

LUCKY WIPED down the mahogany counter and thought about when he rode his bike earlier, and Belle's lithe body pressed against his back

"You gonna spit shine that thing?" His grizzly business partner, Geezer, asked as he stacked beer bottles in the cooler underneath.

"Might."

Two men in leather jackets snatched seats at the bar. He handed them each a bottle of Bud. His friends, Thorny and Havoc came in nearly every night.

"Something eating at you … like maybe the gal in our stockroom?" Geezer asked.

"Nope." It was none of his business.

"The redhead from last night?" Thorny perked up, interested.

"She's a looker. If I weren't a happily married man, might ask her out myself." Geezer winked.

"Thought you kicked the gal out last night. You two connect later?"

Even if Lucky wanted to, he couldn't take advantage of anyone down on their luck.

"Well, she's helping out here tonight." Geezer stood beside Lucky, holding a metal shaker. He picked up a bottle. "Running low on vodka."

"I'll get it." Lucky could use a break from these jokers.

"I'll bet you will." Snickers followed as Lucky entered the storage room.

Belle stood on a ladder reaching for the top shelf.

"How's it going?" he asked, fighting his desire to wrap his hands around her and pull her close.

She turned. "Just finished inventory."

"Already?" He glanced at the clock. Taking the clipboard from her hand, he put it on the shelf.

"Ever serve drinks?" He grabbed a case of vodka.

"Not in a saloon." She moved down the ladder and stood next to him, placing one hand on her hip. "Would that be a problem?"

"Nope. Just take orders, deliver drinks, and collect money."

"Think I could handle that. How are the customers?"

"Most are mellow, especially the old-time bikers." They might have been rougher in their younger years. "Occasionally, we get somebody who has to prove he's tough, but folks usually get along. Drink beer or hard liquor, talk Harleys, play music on the jukebox."

"You like running this place?"

"I'd rather work on Harleys, but it's okay." He shrugged, wishing he'd kept that idea to himself. "Anyway, use these order pads for their drinks." He handed her a stack.

"How do I keep track of people and their orders?"

"Number the orders with the tables. There's a schematic taped inside the caddy."

"What about prices?" She pushed a strand of hair behind her ear. He followed the curve of her finger drawing his attention to her slender neck. Her blouse showed a hint of cleavage.

He sucked in a deep breath and quickly grabbed the caddy out of the safe. "The list of prices is right next to the table numbers. Draft's two dollars. Bottled beer three. Cocktails vary. This attaches to the tray. Hold your hand flat underneath." He modeled the position and passed the tray to her.

"Like this?" She copied his action

"You're a pro."

"Not yet, but I'll be before the night's done."

"You don't lack confidence." He appreciated her bravado. "There's a total of forty dollars in fives and ones to make change. If anyone pays with a credit card bring it to me."

They strolled out together. Lucky stepped behind the bar.

"Seein' as you have plenty of help, I'll be in the office ordering next month's liquor," Geezer said.

Belle delivered drinks to a table in the corner. "Crazy Little Thing Called Love" blared from the jukebox. Her foot tapped as she collected money from the customers, went over to a couple, and took their order. Then she moved to a group of middle-aged customers and shimmied as she found her way to the bar. "Great song," she said, swaying to the music.

He couldn't take his eyes off her.

"You ever been crazy in love?"

"Never." Five years ago, he had thought he was in love. After an argument with his live-in girlfriend, he rode off without her and had an accident. It'd been bad enough that he'd wrecked his motorcycle and lay in the hospital, his leg broken in three places. He thought his girlfriend would stick around, not text to say she didn't want to doctor a man she no longer loved. That sealed his mind. Real love didn't exist. Thinking about that dreadful episode left a sour taste in his mouth.

"You all right?" Belle's voice startled him.

"Fine."

"Then I'll take five long-necks and three drafts.

He pulled her order. Belle loaded the mugs on her tray and struggled to pick it up. Her hold slipped. A bottle wobbled off.

Havoc caught it. "Here you go."

"Thanks." She blushed and walked away slowly.

"Born to be Wild," played. As Lucky poured drinks, his focus continually drifted to wherever she was. She chatted with customers and impressively handled the orders with only a few mishaps.

She set the tray on the counter and ordered. "Two bottles of Bud, a Rob Roy, Lemon Drop Martini, and Sex on the Beach." She crinkled her brow. "Is that really a drink?"

"Sure is." He set the beers on the tray, picked up the shaker placing it on the counter, and added a scoop of ice. "You start with cranberry and orange juice." He picked up two bottles. "Then add vodka and peach liqueur." He used a shot glass to measure.

"Doesn't look hard." She stared at his hands.

"Once it's shaken, I pour the drink into a glass and top it off with a cherry." He dropped the fruit between his fingers.

"Sounds delicious." She ran her tongue along her top lip. "Sometime soon, I'll have to try Sex on the Beach," her low and sultry tone didn't help his overactive imagination.

He glanced at the clock. "Since it's past midnight, after you deliver those drinks, go back in the office and total your tickets with Geezer. When you're done, have a seat at the bar, and I'll make you that cocktail."

"You're on," she said and hurried off.

Ten minutes later, "Free Bird" played as she approached the bar. Havoc pushed his drink and napkin aside to give her room.

"Made forty bucks." Her sweet smile made Lucky's breath catch.

He handed her two more twenties. "Appreciate your help."

"This should buy my bus ticket."

Initially, he'd planned to pay for it. Still might. "Let me know what you think of Sex on the Beach." Saying the name brought up elicit images of her.

She took a sip. "Yummy."

Lucky cleared glasses from the right side of the bar to keep from staring at her.

"You don't look like a biker chick. What brings you to this bar?" Havoc asked her.

"I *literally* stumbled into this place

"Yeah. Saw Lucky haul you out."

"Not one of my finer moments." She swirled her straw around her drink, round and round.

"We've all had 'em." Havoc nudged her. "Even him. Heard you two went riding. Lucky's Harley is old. Got a new dresser if you need a lift."

"What's a dresser?" Belle asked.

"A bike made with all the extras. It's especially comfortable for long rides."

Lucky wanted to grab his friend by the shirt. Belle was *his*. He shook his head. *His?* Where'd did that crazy thought come from?

Belle looked at Lucky. "Maybe some other time. How long have you mortals been riding?"

"Mortals?" Lucky raised a brow.

"Men," she quickly said.

"Don't recall when I wasn't riding." Havoc held up a finger and motioned for another draft.

"I started out with dirt bikes as a kid," Thorny chimed in from the other side of Havoc. "You own one?"

"Not yet, but after being on the back of Lucky's, I'd consider it." Belle sipped her drink, flicked her tongue along her lips, and downed the rest of her drink. "Never worked on a motorcycle, but I've rebuilt drone engines."

"Had one of those. Flew it into a tree." Havoc grinned. "Wasted two-hundred dollars."

Lucky found drones a nuisance.

Thorny ordered her another drink.

A burning ignited inside his chest. He looked down. His hand clutched the soda gun, and he put it in place.

"Are your motorcycles similar to Lucky's?" she asked.

"His is a Knucklehead. The rocker boxes on the engine resemble a knuckle." Havoc put his hand on her shoulder. "You have no idea what I'm talking about, right?"

"Not really, but I'd like to learn." Her eyes sparkled with interest.

"It'd be easier to explain with pictures," Lucky spoke up. "Got plenty of manuals in the garage I could show you." Lucky's grandfather had collected them. Said he'd thought about opening a Harley shop but ended up going in with his friend on this bar. He missed the old coot.

"I've got a 1966 Shovelhead," Thorny said. "Be more 'n' happy to take you for a ride."

Lucky stopped wiping down the bar and waited to hear her answer.

"Can't. I'm leaving Monday." She shrugged. "But thanks. If I'm ever back in town, I'll take you up on your offer."

Geezer came in from the back office. "You've closed all week, so it's my turn."

Lucky wanted to hug the old guy. "Thanks. Ready to go, Belle?"

"Yes." She slid off the barstool. "Thanks for the drink."

"Was my pleasure." Thorny smiled as he winked at her.

He'd like to knock that smile off his face. His teeth ached from clenching his jaw. This awkward twinge of jealousy didn't sit well with Lucky.

CHAPTER 10

Belle hadn't slept much last night because she kept thinking about the mixed messages Lucky gave her. His eyes had followed her as she moved around the bar, which made her ninety-eight percent sure he was attracted. She thought she saw a flare of jealousy when his friend offered to give her a ride on his new dresser.

Once they got back to his place, he walked her to his apartment door and didn't attempt anything. She was hoping he'd kiss her. Had she misinterpreted his interest?

Darn Serenity for planting the idea of kissing a mortal. If Belle were more spontaneous like her friend, she might have initiated the kiss. She imagined his wicked mouth commanding her attention and inciting heat.

Her lips tingled from the thought.

It was half-past nine a.m.

No sense dwelling on what didn't happen. She'd wanted an adventure far from Cupid's Corner, and that's exactly what she got.

Sun shone through the blinds, and she closed them. She pulled on a pink T-shirt, pulled out a pair of jeans with holes in the knees, slipped on boots she'd worn last night. She headed toward the house and knocked.

Lucky opened the wooden door. Seeing his clean-shaven face had her yearning to reach out and brush her fingertips along his chin. "I'm making blueberry pancakes. Wanna help?

"I'm not much of a cook." She focused on his broad shoulders.

"I'll teach you." He slipped an apron over her T-shirt.

Reading the front of the apron, "I May Be Wrong, But It's Highly Unlikely," she laughed, "You picked the perfect one for me."

"If you say so." He stepped toward the kitchen counter with her following.

"See Lucky loaned you my apron." Gran plopped into a kitchen chair on the end.

"Hope you don't mind I borrowed it, Mrs. O'Sullivan?"

"Call me Gran."

"Sure, Gran."

"Quit chatting and earn your keep." Lucky winked.

"Thought I did last night." That didn't come out right. She felt her cheeks heat.

"Not even." He handed her a measuring cup and scooted a canister of flour along the counter. "I need one and a half cups."

She dipped the cup inside.

"Use a knife to level it like this." He put his hand over hers and used the utensil to slide the excess flour into the canister. "Dump it into this bowl with baking powder, salt, sugar. Then fill it halfway and add the rest."

With him behind her, the sink to her right, and the stove to her left, the tight space had her aware of his woodsy cologne. She dumped in the flour. White particles wafted through the air.

"I'll give you ten points for enthusiasm. You ever crack an egg?" His breath tickled her neck.

"Does hard boiled count?"

"Not in pancakes." He stepped back, opened the fridge, and got out a carton of eggs, milk, and butter. "Watch and learn."

He cracked the egg.

"Are you supposed to leave in the shell?" She pointed to a large piece.

"Nope," he fished it out, added milk, and melted butter.

"Whisk the ingredients. I'll heat the griddle."

The utensil clacked as it hit the sides of the bowl. She stirred and stirred and stirred.

He added a big handful of blueberries. "That's good. Rinse the whisk in the sink, and I'll help you with the batter."

He moved behind her, his large calloused hands were once again touching hers.

"Pour a round circle to fill about a quarter of the griddle like this. Your turn." He released his hold.

She spilled a king-sized glob. "Oh, no."

"That'll be mine."

"Think I'd better take a seat and let the pro do his magic." She handed him the bowl.

"I wasn't gonna have you wash the dishes, but now—"

"Guests don't do dishes," Gran called.

"I like your grandmother." Belle sat to Gran's right. She thought she heard Lucky mumble, "Suck up."

Farryn strolled in wearing jeans and a cute peasant style blouse. "Anyone make coffee?"

"There's a fresh pot on the counter. Be a doll, and top off mine," Gran said.

"You want any coffee?" she asked Belle.

"Yes, please." Belle could use an extra jolt of energy.

His sister set a cup in front of Belle and scooted to a seat on the opposite side. Belle added generous amounts of creamer, heaped in several spoonfuls of sugar, and stirred.

"Would you care for a little coffee with that sugar?" Lucky stood behind her holding a platter piled high with golden brown cake.

"Maybe a smidgen." Just for that comment, she dolloped in more granules.

"HOW MANY PANCAKES?" Lucky asked Belle. She seemed far too comfortable in this setting, which troubled him for some odd reason.

"Two small ones."

He flipped them onto her plate, nabbed four for himself, and handed off the platter to his sister. Belle drenched her pancakes with syrup.

"How'd it go last night?" Gran asked.

"Great. Lucky let me serve drinks."

"You're nuts. Some of the guys there can be kinda scary." Farryn frowned

Lucky wasn't surprised by that comment. He'd discouraged his sister from going to the bar after dark.

"Not when you ask them about their motorcycles. They could go on for hours." Her expression softened. She'd enjoyed interacting with the customers. Funny, but the only thing he recalled about last night was how her hips swayed to the music.

Lucky helped himself to more pancakes and polished them off quickly. "I gotta rebuild my bike's carburetor."

"Mind if I join you?" She tilted toward him.

"I wouldn't if I were you. Last time I tried to help him, I broke several fingernails." Farryn lifted her eyes.

"Thought you did that scrolling on your phone."

"They could go on like this for hours." Gran stood and walked toward the back door. "I've got weeding to do."

"And I've got a term paper to write. Let me know what

happens with the woman your aunt knew." She scurried toward her room.

"I'm pretty good with mechanical things." Belle gave him an impish grin.

"A carburetor's dirty work, plus you'll be inhaling strong cleaning fluids."

"Don't mind. I'm kind of a geek that way."

"You're a geek?" He envisioned her in tight overalls. "I can lend you goggles to enhance your inner nerd."

"I'd like that." She finished her cup of coffee. Her long hair might get in the way.

"Better put your hair back in a band." He grabbed a covered band from the bathroom. "Here you go."

As they walked to the garage, she secured her hair in a ponytail. He motioned to his messy workbench. "Welcome to O'Sullivan's garage. My grandfather's legacy." He pointed to the fist-sized carburetor inside a metal pan. "Took the part off this morning and soaked it in cleaner."

"I'm surprised I didn't hear you banging around in here." She picked up a rebuilding kit and pulled out the instructions. "Bet you can't wait to take it apart." Her face brimmed with enthusiasm.

"You're joking, right? Carburetors are a pain."

She scanned the paper, poured out the box onto an old cookie sheet, and started separating parts. "This is fascinating."

No, she was fascinating. He handed her a pair of work gloves. "You'll need these."

"Thanks."

He pulled a torn and tattered Knucklehead manual from a shelf and turned to the page on carburetors. "This book's saved my hide plenty of times."

"You? Weren't you born with a wrench in your hand?"

"Pretty much." He couldn't resist tugging on her ponytail.

"What's that for?"

"Just wanted to see if your hair's as soft as it looks. It is, by the way."

"Once we finish, think you could take me out for a ride?"

"Sure." He wouldn't mind having her on the back.

"It says to remove the screws on the float bowl." She snagged a screwdriver from his toolbox next to the bench.

He pulled down a plastic tray from a shelf and added a paper towel. "I've learned the hard way to keep every nut and bolt in order." He used a sharpie, circled the screws, and labeled them.

She tapped off the bowl like a pro.

"Where'd you learn to do that?"

"Self-taught. Growing up I pretty much dismantled any toy I ever got. Had to check out the inside mechanisms. And paid the price with countless timeouts in my room." She gave a partial smile. "But I didn't mind."

"I remember my dad being livid when I took apart the toaster. It smoked when he tried to use it." That was before his mother left and his dad filled his free time drinking.

"Where does your father live now?" she asked.

"He died." His mood soured at the memory.

"I'm sorry." She gave him a sympathetic look. "Mind if I ask what happened?"

"It's not a real happy story. He drank too much."

"That's so sad." She put her hand on top of his.

He couldn't stand being pitied. "Hand me the wrench so I can tighten this bolt."

She did quickly. "My parents just celebrated their thirtieth wedding anniversary."

"You've had the perfect life." He didn't mean to sound edgy.

"It's been okay." She pressed her lips together, proof he wasn't the only one with family issues.

He poured fluid in the container. "Use a brush to get off all the gunk." They cleaned side by side.

"It's done. Hand me the screwdriver, and I'll add in the float."

"You've done this before."

"On a much smaller version."

He watched her hold her tongue go to the side of her mouth as she tightened a screw. Smart, and oh so alluring using his tools, she installed new jets. Desire zinged through his body.

Shit, she's leaving. "You sure you can't call in sick tomorrow? Got plenty of projects in here to tinker with."

"Can't. Just got a new position a few weeks ago." Her shoulders stiffened.

"Doing what?"

"Testing virtual reality projects. Top secret ones." Her thick ponytail bounced as she replaced the last gasket.

"Right. Next you'll say you work for the C.I.A."

"How'd you guess?" She stopped and smirked at him.

"Must be that dark suit and sunglasses."

"Smart aleck. Anyway, isn't it time you started up that bike?"

"Yes, ma'am. It usually takes tweaking to get the engine running smoothly." He got on, and it whirled.

Belle scanned through pages in the manual. "Did you check the petcock to make sure the fuel line is on?"

"It's on. The fuel line is hooked up. What else could it be?" Frustrated, he wanted to be riding. "I'll double check the vacuum line." He found it loose and fixed it. "You wanna try to get it to start?"

"Do I ever?" she hopped on, gave it two soft prime kicks, turned on the ignition, and gave it a hard kick. The engine roared.

"You did it." His bike sounded better than ever. "You have quite a mechanical knack. Wonder if you're any good at body work or welding?"

"Don't know. Never tried it before, but I'm willing to learn."

"If you're ever back in town, maybe you can assist me." He expected her to smile, not turn away. "Let's take a test drive."

"Where to?" she asked.

"Tranquility Lake. I'll make us sandwiches and grab towels." He stopped. "You do swim, don't you?"

"Like a sailfish." She gave him a saucy grin.

CHAPTER 11

Arriving at Tranquility Lake. Lucky admired how the sunlight brought out red highlights in Belle's long wavy hair. "This way." He led her along a trail past the picnic area where families filled the tables. "Forgot this place gets busy once church lets out. If you're up to a short hike in the hills before we swim, I know a perfect place for lunch."

"Okay." She pursed her bow-shaped lips, the same lips that tempted him since he watched her savor her pancakes.

They turned off at a dirt path. A pair of men wearing cargo pants approached from the other direction and waved as they passed them on the left side.

"It's pretty here. Do you know what kind of tree that is?"

"California sycamore." He stopped, pulled off a leaf, and handed it to her. "Their large leaves offer extra shade in the summer."

A lizard skittered underneath a bush as they wound their way along the trail.

"Race you to the top of the hill." Before he could get his legs moving, she bolted ahead. Her ponytail hitting her back, her arms pumping, her boots hitting the ground quickly.

It took him several seconds to sprint. A burst of power kicked in stronger than downing an energy drink. He might pay for this action with an aching knee later. Never one to back down from a challenge, he picked up his pace, concentrating on the path in front of him. His lungs starved for oxygen as he made it to the top of the hill.

Belle rested against a tree, wearing a smug, satisfied grin. "What do I get for winning?"

Trying to remain cool and collected when his mouth twitched for more. "Would've beat you on that run if you hadn't given yourself a head start."

"I doubt that."

"You're pretty confident," he said.

"Why wouldn't I be? I won."

"And you'd never gloat." He clasped her hand—softness against his callouses. "Come see this view." He walked her toward the embankment. "What do you think of the city?"

"Amazing. Where's your house?"

"The white buildings are the Tranquility Mall. My street's on the other side of the boulevard. From this angle, you can't see the house."

"You promised lunch. I'm starving."

"Why am I not surprised?" Most dates ate like a bird

around him. Not Belle. "This way." They settled at a bench under a shady tree with initials carved into the trunk. He'd never had that kind of meaningful relationship. He wasn't the type of guy that good girls fell for. An outsider. A biker. Never fitting in with the popular kids from high school. It didn't help that his father loved to drink, and on any night, he never knew what to expect. His mechanic father once owned an auto shop but eventually lost it.

She cleared her throat.

He grabbed the large paper sack from his backpack. "Brought you a soda." He tapped on the top and popped the lid for her. "Made you a cheese sandwich, mine's ham."

"Thanks." She sn a bite and gave him an impish smile. "You're pretty handy in the kitchen."

"I like to cook, sort of create my own recipes."

She nudged him with her shoulder. "You can make meals for me any day.

"You're a natural with directions, yet you don't cook. Why is that?"

"The kitchen was off limits."

"I blew up a toaster. What'd you do?"

"Let's just say my folks didn't care for the chemical concoctions I created." She pulled in a deep breath and slowly released it. "They banished me to the field behind the house."

"Giving you hours and hours to master your scientific skills. I imagine you could do just about anything if you set your mind to it." He sipped his soda, wondering what other secret abilities she had. "Ever think about having your own business?"

"Not really. How 'bout you?"

"Every day. I've thought about opening a motorcycle shop on the lot next to the bar." His grandfather had deeded the property to him.

"What's stopping you?"

"Money." At least he'd finally paid off the last of his medical bills.

"If you ever get that motorcycle shop, you'll have to hire me."

"Deal." He shook her hand.

They finished their food.

"I'm ready for that swim."

"You're on." He couldn't wait to see her in a bathing suit.

BELLE LEFT the lake's changing room in her borrowed one-piece swimsuit with a fancy crocheted peekaboo effect connecting a bikini like top and bottom.

Lucky waited for her under an oak tree. "Hey, princess." He stepped closer, revealing his bare chest with a splattering of dark hair. Toned, not overly buff, lean, lanky and, gorgeous. The intensity in his gaze caused her inner core to tingle.

"We'll put our things over there." He motioned to the empty section of the sandy shore to the right, away from the lifeguard station where the families gathered. "Hope the water's not too cold."

"If it is, I'm not going in."

"We'll see about that." His lips quirked, and those devilish dimples appeared.

"You threatening me?" Pebbles crunched under her flip-flops as she strode next to him.

"Who me?" Lucky spread a throw blanket on the sandy ground. "Have a seat."

She dropped to her knees, watching him as he sidled in next to her.

"You're pretty fair. Better use this." He tossed her a bottle of sunscreen.

"Water resistant. Good choice." She sprayed her arms and legs and tentatively spritzed her face.

"Stay put. Hold up your hair, and I'll get your back." He snagged the sunscreen bottle out of her hand, drizzled her back with a cool mist. Then he applied lotion to his chest. "Mind returning the favor?"

"Not at all." She coated his waist while comparing it to his wide shoulders. What would he do if she decided to massage those muscles?

"You up for that swim?" He offered his hand, helping her rise. Heat flickered where their fingers touched.

Reaching the water, she wiggled her toes at the edge. "It's not that cold."

"Last one in is a rotten egg." He rushed into the water until he was deep enough to swim.

"Wait for me," she called. Able to see his head, she swam behind him, dove under, and popped up in front of him. She couldn't resist splashing his face.

"You're gonna get it for that." He reached for her and missed.

Swimming about a yard from him, she came up. "Can dish it out but can't take it."

"Thought I was a good swimmer, but you're quite a fish."

"One you'll never catch." She swam toward the shore and stood where her feet touched the bottom.

He caught up to her, turned her to face him, keeping his arms on her shoulders.

She held her breath for a beat as he gazed at her. Then his mouth brushed against her lips. My gosh, his lips were warm and welcoming. Her arms roped around his neck, pressing his body against hers. A shiver of heat shimmied down her spine.

"Been dying to do that," his voice crooned.

"What took you so long?"

"Are you always so sassy?" He leaned down, his tongue teased the corner of her mouth, and he deepened the kiss.

Her lips tingled. Were all human kisses as addicting as Lucky's? That would explain why Cupids forbid mortal contact. Tempted to initiate the next caress, her stomach growled. She playfully pushed her hands against his chest. "I'm hungry. Is there anything else left to eat in your backpack?"

He laughed, deep in his belly. "You're impossible, princess. Let's dry off, and then I'll take you to the snack bar."

"Only if you're buying." She poised on the blanket with her arms around her knees.

"And if I don't." He unzipped his backpack, threw her a towel and got one for himself, all the while admiring her.

"Then I won't share." She stood.

"If I were you, I'd wait 'till I had food in my hand before I said any more."

"Good thing you're not me." She walked next to him.

At the stand, he said, "You're lucky I'm in a good mood. What do you want?"

She stared at the menu. Onion rings. Mozzarella sticks. Popsicles. "Hmm … I'll have a frozen banana dipped with sprinkles."

"You sure like sweet things."

"You mean like you?" She batted her eyelashes.

He chuffed and ordered a cheeseburger, fries, soda. "Next time we're back here, it's your treat."

"Works for me." Chances she'd return were slim. Sneaking to Earth had been risky. Sun glimmered off a white gash from his thigh down to his knee "How'd you get that scar?"

"Bike accident."

"Bet that hurt. What happened?" She bit into her treat. Banana and chocolate practically sang in her mouth.

"One minute I was happily riding along. The next, a car clipped me from behind, and I careened off the road."

She could hear angst in his voice. "Must've been awful. I once broke my wing … arm falling from a tree."

"Your wing arm? Bet you climbed to the top of a tree with cardboard wings and tried to fly?"

"How'd you guess?" Did he suspect something? She glanced behind her shoulders. Bare skin. No marks where her wings usually unfurled.

"Farryn tried the same thing. Gran caught her making her debut flight off the top of the avocado tree in the backyard."

"Did she break her arm?"

"Sure did. She wore her neon pink cast like a badge. What color was yours?"

"Purple. It's my favorite color, in case you were wondering."

"I wasn't." He chuckled.

At their blanket, she lowered herself.

"Hold this." He handed her his soda.

She took a sip.

"Are you always so grabby?" He moved in beside her and snatched back his drink. When his fingers brushed hers, kinetic energy arced back and forth between them.

He stared at her with a lifted brow.

Would he kiss her again? She sure hoped so.

Instead, he got out his burger and bit into it.

"Bet your favorite song's "Born to be Wild," she said.

"Nope. It's "I Won't Back Down."

"Love that song. Wish I were like that person." Especially when it came to her grandmother.

"You don't back away from a challenge, not even when a malicious bartender tosses you out." His eyes held hers.

Embarrassed, she changed topics. "What is the best place you've ever seen?"

"Yellowstone. You ever been?"

"Can't say I have?"

"You should go. Nothing but wilderness for miles. Bison, bears, occasionally a moose." His voice sounded wistful.

"Didn't take you for a tree hugger."

"Never hugged a tree in my life. Okay, little miss snarky, what's your favorite place?"

"Can't pick just one?" She got up and threw her stick in the trash. "I'll take another swim and think it over." And she took off, rushing through the shallow shore, diving in the deeper waters, reveling in the coolness, she held her breath and stayed under. When she came up for air, she glanced toward their spot, not surprised to see it empty.

"You always run when you don't want to answer a question?" He glided close to her, his brown eyes flecked with golden speckles.

"Did an arowana fish just jump out of the water?"

"A what?"

"Race you to the buoy and back." She paddled fast, hearing the splashing behind her. Lucky must be getting close, but she kept swimming and touched the floating red and white ball. "I win."

"Not exactly," he said from behind her. "It's to the buoy and back." He tagged the float and swam toward the shore.

She caught up to him, standing in water up to his hips.

"What took you so long?" Water glistened off his body. Holy Zeus, the guy was hot.

"You do realize I let you win."

"You're delusional." He kissed her with a little tenderness and a whole lot of zeal.

When he stopped kissing her, she'd forgotten where she was. Several seconds in the sun and she noticed the lapping water along the shoreline and a crow cawing overhead.

"Let's get dressed." He dropped his hold, not appearing the least bit frazzled. "I'd like to stop at a fruit stand before we head back to the house."

"Sure." She adored riding with him. What a shame she couldn't stay for a few more days.

CHAPTER 12

Most women hated getting dirt under their fingernails. Hell, most women couldn't tell the difference between a fan clutch and torque wrench. Belle was unique. Thanks to her help, the engine ran perfectly. It felt right to have her arms tightly around him as he drove along West Road.

He slowed the bike, pulled off into a dirt driveway on the right, and stopped in front of Sammy's Stand—a rectangular building with a long green and white awning.

She immediately hopped off and walked to the stand.

He paused next to her as she picked up three lemons from a bin on the table. With two in one hand, one in the other, she tossed the fruit in the air and juggled.

"Let me guess. You once worked as a circus clown."

A lemon dropped to the ground, rolled past the stand,

and underneath a picnic table. "See what you did. Looks like you're buying that one."

Her flippant attitude made him laugh. "Already planned on it. Gran makes the best lemonade." Gran's sweet lemonade brought back memories of his childhood. Happy times escaping his bickering parents and visiting the safe haven his grandparents created. Often, he'd wind up the garage helping Gramps with his latest motorcycle project.

"Hey! Who's your friend?" The stocky middle-aged owner brought him back to the present.

Lucky shook the man's hand. "Belle, this is Sammy. He's operated this stand for as long as I can remember."

"Nice to meet you."

"Make yourself useful and snag that wayward lemon," Lucky said to keep from staring at her berry-colored lips.

She gave a mock huff and headed toward the picnic table several yards south.

"Haven't seen your grandmother since bingo night. What's she been up to?"

"You know Gran. Always busy." He watched Belle as she bent over to snatch the lemon. Hot damn, she had a nice ass.

"Here you go?" She handed him the lemon.

He fingered a basket of strawberries. "Too bad it isn't apple season. In case you were wondering, apple pie's one of my favorites."

"I wasn't." The corners of her mouth lifted as she put one hand on her hip.

Lucky snatched two oranges, threw them in the air,

bobbled them with his palms up. Both fell to the ground and rolled under the stand. "Show me how to juggle."

"Start with one. Toss it back and forth. Get a feel for the shape and weight."

He tossed it easily.

"Keep your hands steady and pick up another orange. Hold it in your hand. When you toss it, and it reaches the top of its arc, toss the other one." He did it twice and dropped both.

"Teaching you is too much work." Her eyes twinkled.

"Smart aleck. Guess I'll have to practice on my own." Might be a fun trick to do in the bar when it's slow. "You thirsty."

She nodded.

"Grab yourself a soda." He snagged a Coke and paid.

She sifted through the bucket, pulled out a root beer, and shook the can to rid the ice clinging to the sides. "My fingertips feel colder than the top of Mt. Olympus."

"Are they now?" Sometimes she sounded as if she came from another country. He put his soda down and rubbed her hands, noting how dainty they were in comparison to his. "Better?"

"Much."

Let's take a break over there." He motioned to a bench five-yards away. Popping the soda's top, he took a big guzzle. "That hits the spot."

She pulled her tab. Soda fizzled out of the hole and hissed. She dropped the can.

"Next time make sure to tap the top to get rid of the bubbles. Here, take mine." He gave her his Coke and picked up her soda, tossing it to the trash.

She sipped the drink. "This is refreshing. I'll share."

He finished the rest, moved onto the bench, and snaked his arm around her. "Hope you'll learn more about your aunt today."

"So do I. She must've done something dreadful to be disowned." Belle looked away.

"Any idea what?"

"I've searched through old family photos but couldn't find her.

"That is odd. Tell me about your family."

"I have an older and younger sister."

"Are they pretty like you?" Belle was gorgeous.

She blushed. "They're blond, blue-eyed, and petite like my mother."

"You inherit your mysterious eyes from your father?"

"That's the quagmire. According to my grandfather, I take after a great uncle."

"Are you and your grandfather close?"

"He gets me. Always has." She wrinkled her brows. "As caring as he is, it doesn't make sense that he'd go along with his wife and pretend his daughter never existed."

"Why didn't you ask him?"

"Because after I called my mom, she shut me down. If my own mom won't talk to me, I doubt anyone will. Plus, she made it clear that I was not to talk about Zinnia with anyone."

"You don't strike me as the kind of person who'd cower to anyone." She certainly hadn't when they first met.

"I usually don't, but when my mom gets that way, it's best to pick my battles.

"Except, you didn't give up."

She gave him a beaming smile. "The next day, I found my aunt's address and decided to leave Friday night. It was a good plan until—" She let out a long breath.

"You entered my bar. Are you still thinking about that night?"

"Not at all. Because of you, I'm a phone call away from learning about Zinnia." She kissed his cheek.

"What if it turns out to be a dead end?" He slipped his arm around her shoulders and pulled her closer. "Will you talk with your grandfather when you get back?"

"Probably at some point."

"What about your grandmother? Zinnia is her daughter, too."

Belle shook her head. "She and my mom are close. Plus, she's mean and opinionated and—"

"A bitch."

"You've met her?" Belle squinted at him.

"I've met her type."

"I'm sure you have working the bar. Anyway, I can't give up. I can be rather tenacious."

"I've noticed." He couldn't resist pressing his lips against hers. They kissed for a while.

She sighed when he pulled away. Then she cocked her head and gazed at him. "Enough about me. Tell me about your childhood."

"Gran and Farryn are great. My parents weren't exactly ideal."

"What do you mean?"

He swallowed hard. "Growing up, I never knew if I'd walk into an explosive fight or people who couldn't keep their hands off each other." His parents were either fiery tempered or cold. Before his mother left, they'd turned distant, ignoring both he and his sister. He fought off the sadness that hit him deep in his gut. "What about your parents?"

"They love me, but it's obvious they wish I acted more like my sisters. They don't understand why I love tinkering with mechanical things." Tears formed, and she blinked them away. "Holy Zeus, I'm ruining my hard ass image." Then she winked, looking brash.

"Sorry, princess, but you ruined that image when you got in a fight with your high heels."

She glared at him. "I'd had a bad night."

He lifted a hand, gently ran a finger down the side of her cheeks and tipped her chin up toward him. His lips met hers lightly and pulled away. "Let's head back."

"Who made you boss?"

"Me." He got up and snatched her hand. Threading their fingers, it seemed right, almost natural.

"And here I was starting to like you."

"You like me plenty." He kissed her.

AT NINE P.M., Lucky grabbed a handful of Easy Rider magazines and joined Belle at the outdoor table.

"Provocative cover," she said, motioning to a bikini-clad woman draped across a motorcycle.

"What can I say? Sexy women sell magazines. You ever model?" She was certainly pretty enough.

"Me? Not hardly."

"You should. You're way hotter in a swimsuit than this gal." Remembering her at the lake, dripping wet in her one piece, his body stirred. He picked up another magazine and glanced at the title page. "Check out Tech Garage. This issue shows how to rebuild clutches."

"Really. Let me see." She snatched the magazine from him, her eyes bright as a Fourth of July sparkler.

His cell rang.

She stiffened.

"It's from Friendly City." He pushed the green button and handed her the phone. "Here you go."

"Hello." She got up and paced to the avocado tree, back to the patio. "Yes … I see … Troy with a T … Do you recall where they moved?"

Lucky secretly hoped her aunt lived nearby. That would give her an easy excuse to visit Tranquility. He'd like to see what she could do with the engine pieces he had in a box. Hell, he'd like to take her out again.

"Thanks, you've been a big help ... I will." She sat next to him at the table and slid him his cell. Her expression pensive.

"Well, what did the woman say?"

"Aunt Zinnia married a local, Troy Anderson, and at some point moved away from Friendly City. Couldn't say for sure where they went. At least I've got a name."

"Find Troy Anderson," he spoke into his phone.

"I found forty listings," the computer voice said.

"Let's use Gran's computer. The images will be bigger." He led her inside.

She took the computer chair, and he pulled another from the kitchen. "Click on Facebook."

Farryn's page came up. She scrolled to his image and clicked. "What a cheesy sweater."

"My sister set up the page."

"And you let her?" Belle gave an impish grin.

Lucky didn't tell her how relentless his sister had been. It was easier to give in.

Belle typed in Troy Anderson. They started at the top and clicked on various people. A white-haired man—too old. A teenage boy—too young. A scantily clad lady—not likely.

"Try adding Friendly City."

"No matches." She slumped down.

"You'll find her." He stood and put his hands on her shoulders, lightly rubbing them. "Try the white pages."

"There are thousands of hits."

"Narrow it to Southern Cal."

"One-hundred-seventy-one. Still too broad." Her pursed lips didn't set well with him.

"Want a beer?" he asked, figuring the alcohol might help her relax.

"Okay," she continued working on the computer. "This is too frustrating. When I get home, I'll have access to the Book of Relationships and probably find info." She tilted back in her chair.

"Book of Relationships?"

"Umm, my friend has this extensive genealogy program." She glanced away from him.

He handed her a longneck and said, "It's a nice night. Why don't we sit outside for a while?"

"Sounds good to me."

He pulled out a chair for her at the table and positioned his seat inches from hers.

"You've been such a big help." She put her hand on top of his. "I have the name of the man my aunt married, but I really hoped I'd meet her. I still have so many unanswered questions."

"This gives you a good excuse to visit here."

"We'll see. They may have moved to the other side of the states or even to a different country." She said quietly and sipped her beer. "I tend to drink wine, but I like the yeasty flavor of beer. It's like drinking a slightly bitter bread."

"You're cute." He ran his thumb along her chin and leaned over to kiss her, long and leisurely. "When you come back, we could take a tour of the brewery."

"If I'm back."

"You'll be back." He gave her another smoldering kiss.

"And why would I do that?" She teased.

"Besides missing me, I have a hunch you'll still need my help to find your aunt." He pulled her against him.

"Do your hunches usually come true?"

"About this, I'm quite certain I'll see you again." He couldn't resist grinning.

"It's been a long day. Think I'll call it a night." She yawned.

He held her hand and walked her to the door of his studio. The kiss that followed coursed heat throughout his body. "Sweet dreams, Belle," he said and walked into the house.

CHAPTER 13

Belle went to bed early. Still, her mind kept reliving her Earthly experiences with Lucky. He'd appreciated her help with the carburetor, and the fact that he recognized her as an equal thrilled her to no end. Riding on the back of his bike, she trusted him. He made her feel safe.

He was a generous person, offering to take her to Friendly City to find her aunt, allowing her to stay in his place, and entertaining her on his day off. And my gosh, she had a marvelous time at the lake.

The part that troubled her and kept her tossing and turning most of the night was her extreme attraction to him. Not just because of his golden eyes and endearing smile. He drew her in at such an intense level that she struggled with her own core values. Cupids were forbidden to have physical contact with a mortal. They were not supposed to accept … kisses that enflamed her desire.

Holy Chaos. That man could kiss, making her wonder what it'd be like sleeping with him. Except … Cupids shouldn't kiss mortals much less consider having sex with them.

Wound up, Belle stayed up late reading motorcycle magazines and after that tossing and turning. Lucky's imprints were everywhere—from his large bed with its brown and blue plaid comforter—to his Easy Rider poster decorating the wall. Even the alarm clock reminded her of Lucky—solid with large masculine numbers.

After trying to rid her mind of Lucky, she started thinking about Zinnia and her husband, Troy Anderson. Were they still married? Where had they moved? What were they like?

Why had her aunt been banished from the Brooks family?

At some point, well after three, she must have drifted off to sleep. An alarm clock buzzed and woke her.

Eleven-fifteen. That gave her an hour to get ready and eat something before Lucky brought her to the bus station.

Rushing into the shower, she stepped inside the warm steamy water and breathed in the piney scent of Lucky's soap. From now on, whenever she smelled pine trees—she'd think of him. She finished, wrapped a towel around her body, hurried into the bedroom, sifted through the bag of clothing, pulled out a pair of faded jeans and couldn't get the top snapped.

Darn. Those looked comfy.

She found a pair of obsidian-colored jeans with a hole in the knee. A bit loose in the waist, they'd have to do. She must have tried on five T-shirts until she found one that wouldn't show her stomach. A pale pink top fit loose. Perfect.

Checking her reflection in the mirror, she looked presentable.

She thought about her reason for coming to Earth, certain she would've found her aunt by now. At least she knew her uncle's full name. She rushed to the back of the house and knocked on the kitchen door, glad there'd be time to thank his family for their hospitality.

"Hey." Lucky's smile seemed brighter than a diamond in the sun.

Her heart thumped hard and fast in her chest.

"Make yourself a sandwich. Left the stuff out on the counter."

She stared at his lips. Big mistake because she wouldn't mind sneaking in a kiss. Instead, she opened up a hoagie roll, spread mayonnaise and added cheese, lettuce, and tomatoes.

"Want coffee or root beer?" he asked.

"Root beer, please." The fizzy drink reminded her of yesterday's visit to the fruit stand when her can exploded, and Lucky had been kind enough to share his soda.

He twisted off the lid and sat at the table. She joined him.

"How'd you sleep last night?" He slid a can to her and drank his coffee.

"Not that great. The questions about my aunt and uncle

kept whirling around my head." Along with his wondrous kisses.

"At least you're not driving and can nap on the bus." If she were actually riding a bus the whole way home instead of a sunbeam.

"You still leaving today?" His sister strolled into the kitchen and plopped into a chair near the door.

"I have to work tomorrow."

Gran got up from her computer desk, wearing neon pink sweats and a floral shirt. Lucky called her eccentric, Belle considered her colorful. "Did the lady in Friendly Valley contact you last night?"

"She did. Told me my aunt married Troy Anderson." Belle explained that her search supplied little.

"It's a start." Gran wrote his name on a pad of paper. "I'll ask around. You never know if a lead will pop up."

"Thanks."

"Gotta leave for chem lab. The class is a killer." His sister walked to the door. "If you ever make it back this way, stop by, and we'll do lunch."

"That would be nice."

The glint in Lucky's eyes said he was proud of his sister. "We'd better get going, too."

Belle stood. Gran hugged her, her rose scent matched the flowers she grew in her yard. "Good luck with your aunt."

"Thanks for letting me stay here." She'd only been in town a few days, but it seemed like longer.

"It was our pleasure." Gran handed her a sack lunch. "Packed you this, just in case you get hungry."

"You're a doll." Belle embraced the sweet lady.

MELANCHOLY HIT as Belle saw the bus station sign. Her Earthly adventure would be over by sunset. Lucky held her hand inside the boxy station. People waited at benches, sat against the walls, scrolled their cell phones, read newspapers, or slept.

Lucky gave her a printout. "Bought your ticket online."

"You're nice." She kissed his cheek.

"It's the least I could do. You not only helped me in the bar but also with my bike."

"I enjoyed the challenge." The scent of oil and exhaust. His body close to hers as they worked side by side added to her thrilling adventure.

"If you're ever back, I've got a damaged Sportster to restore."

"Sounds fun." The chance of seeing him again—highly doubtful—but she might sneak back.

He walked her over to a long screen with arrivals and departures. "Your bus is already here." His voice sounded flat.

Outside at the loading zone was the waiting vehicle. His hands dwarfed hers. The heat created a warmth deep inside.

"Wish I could stay another day." Enfolding his arms

around her neck, he brushed his lips against her mouth and kissed her slowly, tangling his fingers through her hair. When he pulled away, he reached into his pocket and pulled out a card. "Call me when you're in town."

The bus started up.

"Guess I better get on." She wanted to drag him against her. Instead, she said, "Thanks again for this weekend."

The bus driver cleared his throat. "You coming, miss?"

"Yes." As she stepped inside, she took an empty seat on the right. Seeing him wave, she waved back and said goodbye to her first human friend.

This had been the best adventure ever. She couldn't wait to tell Serenity she'd joined their mortal kissing club.

THREE HOURS LATER, Belle watched out the window as the bus pulled into the Avenal, California Station. Gray concrete surrounded by brown dirt. She went inside and bought a root beer. From now on, root beer would remind her of Lucky.

A sunbeam showed about a quarter mile south of the stop. Thirty minutes and she'd be home in Cupid's Corner. Now that she had Troy Anderson's name, she planned to arrive at work early and search the Book of Relationships.

Might as well eat the sack lunch Gran packed. My gosh, Belle liked that lady. She pulled out a peanut butter and jelly sandwich and devoured it. Polished off carrot sticks and a bag of chips. Still hungry, she found a heart-shaped cookie at the bottom of the bag. How sweet! Literally.

Dust approached. The sky reminded her of a melting Orange Creamsicle. She unzipped the front pocket of her backpack, felt for the invisibility spray, and found the bottle near the bottom of the pocket. A hint of pink tinted the dark blue horizon as she strode south to an empty dirt lot. She liberally sprayed invisibility potion over herself. Her body faded. Running her hand over her backpack, it disappeared.

Daylight dimmed as she shot up the beam and arrived at the top of cumulus clouds. She zoomed through the Calypso Forest, weaved between two shagbark hickory trees and almost snagged her wing. Spotting her five-story apartment building on Bliss Avenue, she flew to the second floor at the side and dashed through the window.

She perched on her bed, invisible. As her body materialized, she glanced at her wrist emblem. Only one message.

Her mother asked her to a barbecue on Sunday if she stayed in town.

Her doorbell made a melodic chime. She parted her cloud-covered door.

"You decided to spend the weekend with Wynton?" Serenity fluttered into the apartment, furled her magenta wings, and relaxed in a chair.

"No." Belle sank into her couch. "We broke up before he left for Lover's Landing."

"Don't tell me you moped around your apartment all weekend?"

"Not at all. The relationship was going nowhere. With him staying in that resort indefinitely, we parted ways without much drama." It turned out to be a win-win for both of them.

"Good for you. Lover's Landing is way over rated anyway." Serenity didn't care for her hometown. "Since you didn't go with him, what *did* you do?" Serenity gave her a you're-telling-me-everything-or-else look."

"Nothing."

"Then why are you blushing?" Serenity eyed her. "You met someone. What's the Cupid's name?"

"You're moonstruck."

"Not at all. Unless—" She stopped, giving Belle a no-you-didn't lift of her brow. "You grilled me about visiting Earth the other night. Did you go?"

"Me?" Belle checked her pink fingernail polish for nicks.

"You little sneak."

No sense lying any longer. "It was a spur of the moment decision."

"Really, Belle? Unlike me, you never do anything on a whim." Serenity said in a sincere tone. "Why'd you go?"

"Hearing you talk about Earth, I wanted an adventure of my own." Actually, after her holiday weekend, adventure became her new favorite word.

"I can relate. When the wanderlust urge hits, you have to go for it." Serenity folded her feet underneath her on the couch and sighed. "My wild ways must be rubbing off on you."

"Let's not take it that far." Belle doubted she could ever be as spirited at her friend.

"Anyway, tell me about the mortal you met. Details." Serenity wouldn't quit badgering her until she got some info.

"Fine." Belle let out a long huff. She needed to talk anyway. Not that she'd mention looking for her aunt. That mystery Belle wanted to keep private.

"Remember the holograph man we were experimenting with at I.P.?"

A smirk lit up Serenity's face. "You mean that hunky human whose voice went haywire?"

"Um … I sorta kissed him."

"Honestly, Belle. You can't sorta kiss a holograph."

"Believe me, he was real." She certainly enjoyed Lucky's tantalizing mouth.

"Based on your blazing cheeks, it must've been scorching."

"Holy Zeus, it was."

"Having your first mortal kiss calls for a celebration." Serenity flicked her fingertips, and coppery dust swirled. Two fluted crystal glasses filled with sparkling pink ambrosia floated to the rose quartz coffee table. "To adventures on Earth."

They clicked their glasses together. Belle sipped the sweet liqueur. "Delicious."

"How'd you end up kissing Mr. Hunky."

"Lucky took me to the lake on the back of his motorcycle, and—"

Serenity fanned her face with her hand. "Being with a rebel's always been a fantasy of mine. Does he have any cutesicle friends?'

Fine as long as she kept her hands-off Lucky. Whoa! Belle needed to squash this idea of rivalry. Serenity never dated her friends' beaus. Except Lucky wasn't her beau.

Belle let out the breath she'd been holding. Lucky's only a human.

"There were a couple of good-looking guys at the bar."

"He works at a bar? Interesting." Serenity wore a goofy grin. "Back to the kiss."

"We went to a lake, frolicked in the water. That's when he ensnared me in his arms and brought his lips against mine." Thinking about him made her core quiver.

"Did you sleep with him?" Serenity sipped her drink.

"Heavens, no. I barely know the guy." Although she knew he liked to tinker with mechanical things, wanted to own his own motorcycle shop someday, and opposite to the Cupids she'd dated, Lucky appreciated her mechanical aptitude.

"You're blushing again. I bet you wouldn't mind seeing him. Let's sneak down to Earth next weekend." Always up for a little fun, she gave Belle a pleading puppy-dog look.

"Give me a couple weeks to recuperate." With Serenity's disregard for rules, partying in Tranquility Valley might not be the smartest idea. Still, bringing her along would be a good excuse to see Lucky. Plus, he might have info on her aunt. Belle held up her empty glass. "Refill."

"By all means."

Serenity tapped on her wrist emblem. "I'm checking for the phases of the moon. It looks like if we go the week after next, the moon should be full."

"Then I'm in." Belle would have more time with Lucky.

They chitchatted for another hour. Serenity talked about the French Mediterranean and swimming nude at Cap d'Adge.

Belle wasn't sure she could ever be that bold. "I'm exhausted. We'll talk tomorrow after work, okay."

"We sure as Hades will." Serenity's wings glittered as she flitted out the cloud covered front door.

CHAPTER 14

Around three p.m., Lucky arrived at the Y.M.C.A. pool. With an hour to swim before he taught a youth polo class, he tossed his towel on a lounge chair and dove into the heated water. The water soothed his knee, taking strain off it.

One lap. His body zipped through the liquid. Reaching the other side and turning underwater he kept going, pushing himself to go faster and faster.

He recalled Belle's interest in mechanical things as she worked next to him in the garage.

Ten laps done. Halfway there.

She swam like a fish. They shared their first kiss in the water.

He kept swimming.

Another day with her would've been nice, but the fact

that she didn't live near him provided plenty of distance; keeping this from turning into a relationship. He'd probably never see her again.

Ten minutes later, he achieved his lap goal. As he stepped out, his knee didn't twinge. Guess working out five times this week instead of the usual three paid off.

A gangly teen and her younger brother walked up. "Hey, coach," Jack said grinning, while his sister's expression remained solemn. At the pool's edge, the boy jumped in cannonball style.

His sister, Jill, tensed. She took on the role of protector. Lucky could relate. Growing up, he'd often felt the need to protect Farryn. Since Lucky began coaching the Wednesday afternoon session, he found the kid's sister at every practice watching from a bench at the side of the pool, rarely smiling. Lucky figured she and her brother led rough lives.

Five more boys came, acknowledged Lucky and dove into the deep end. Another two straggled in.

This coaching position came about because his high school friend wore him down. Lucky agreed to coach for a month. How crazy. After three months, he looked forward to training these boys. He thought back to his freshman year. His life had revolved around polo … until his father died, and he lost all interest in the sport.

He checked the clock.

4:03.

Blowing his whistle, he called, "Ten laps." The boys' arms and legs pumped. Water lapped against the sides of the pool.

He put the eight players through the endurance gauntlet and a series of passing drills and practiced two on two scrimmages.

The boys partnered up for "piggyback rides." The offensive player completed a set of turns with the defensive player on his back. Everyone did well. Then they switch places. About halfway through the drill, Jack started floundering.

Lucky yelled, "It's important to practice correctly. Keep your head up." He glanced over at Jack's sister. She looked like she might jump in the pool fully dressed.

"Time's up." He blew the whistle. The players swam toward the side.

Jill glared at him. He got that Jack was kin, but her tough brother wore a broad grin. If he kept at it, he'd make a great goalie.

"Good job. See you next Wednesday." As each player got out, they gave him a high five.

He showered and got dressed and checked his phone for messages. Seeing none, he might as well head for the Revel Rouser Tavern.

ANOTHER WEEKLY DINNER WITH RELATIVES. Mandatory for as long as Belle could remember, occasionally a relative or two would be absent. Since she'd broken up with Wynton, sooner or later she'd have to tell the family. Awkward, given how they adored him.

Frustrated with her failed attempts to gleam anything from the Book of Relationships about Troy Anderson, she came tonight hoping to gain info about her aunt.

Inside the white-marbled entrance, a portrait of her great, great, grandfather, Rufus Brooks, hung on the wall. His stormy blue eyes seemed to bore right into her as if questioning her presence. His wavy blond hair came to the top of his shoulders, his mouth pressed together. The only resemblance to her—his bow-shaped lips.

"My teacher says if I practice enough, I might shoot love arrows on Earth." A little girl's voice echoed from the dining room, probably her five-year-old niece, Lilly.

Belle fingered her tiger's eye bracelet and entered the spacious dining room. Hopefully, the precocious niece would take the focus off her.

"Where's everyone?" she asked as she sat between her mom and dad. No Grand Dame or G-Dad. No Aunt Anita or Uncle Pete.

"Your grandmother is speaking at a Cupid women's conference. I think your grandfather is either enjoying his peace and quiet or off on an assignment somewhere. Anita and Pete are still at the Calypso Mountain Resort." Her father stood and gave her a big hug.

"The important Cupids are here," Venecia, her younger sister, said.

"Good reply, sis." Belle gave her a thumbs up.

Her older sister, Orchid, passed her a platter of stuffed mushrooms. "Where's Wynton?"

"He got a job in Lover's Landing."

"That's too bad, sweetie. Did he ask you to go with him?" Her mother had worry lines around her mouth.

"Not yet." Belle fiddled with her napkin.

"It's not that far. Maybe you could visit him during your time off next month."

"Maybe." Mom's insinuation was brilliant. In a few weeks, Belle had a vacation coming and planned to head back to Earth. While she hated to lie, having her mother assume she was spending time with Wynton made things easier.

"I think you could do better," Venecia said. "I mean, he's cute, but not exactly the brightest star in the galaxy."

Belle held back a snicker.

The conversation switched to a discussion about Orchid's husband on assignment in Italy. Belle listened, appreciative that the questions about her stopped. Her father waved his hand, and fluted glasses of sparkling juice floated down. Her mother passed out china plates with poached robin's eggs and three-cheese focaccia bread.

Belle traced an etched arrow on the crystal table. Now to direct the topic toward Aunt Zinnia. "What was Dad's family like when you were dating?" She directed her question at her mom.

"His parents were great. His mom has always been such a sweetie."

No sense auguring. Her mother and Grand Dame were tight for some odd reason. She never seemed to notice how

Grand Dame snubbed Belle whenever she got a chance. "What about the others?"

"Your father's siblings are younger than him. They'd often tease me."

"Especially, my youngest sis, Zin—."

Her mother elbowed him.

"Um … Pete bored her with hockey facts." Her dad's face turned pink. "Like most Cupids, he's a Red Wings fan." Odd, the only sports ever mentioned at dinner revolved around archery competitions.

"Time for dessert." Mom flicked her fingertips. Glittery pink dust swirled, materializing on individual bowls of strawberry mousse with whipped cream and drizzled with red sprinkles.

"You have everything ready for your getaway this week-end," Orchid asked her parents.

"I do. I've aired out your old room, Belle. Thanks again for offering to stay," her mom said.

Belle had forgotten her parents were going away Saturday morning. Excellent timing, staying there she'd have time to search the attic. "It's been a while since I've had sister time with Ven."

"Me, too. Wish I didn't have archery practice all day Saturday. But after that, we should go out to eat. Maybe a movie, too."

"Sounds fun. You and Lilly should join us," Belle said.

"I wish I could, but I'm taking Lilly to her cousin Jaimie's birthday party." Orchid patted her daughter's head.

Saturday morning, Belle arrived at the family estate around nine a.m. "Anybody home," she called out. This house hosted generations of Brooks including her grandparents who lived on opposite ends of the mansion.

No one answered.

Good.

She fluttered down the long hall to her former bedroom, the last door on the right, and set her bag on the canopy bed. As a little girl, she used to sit in this very spot and pretend she was a princess riding a unicorn across the land—in search of her true love. What a waste of time that had been.

She stared at the poster of her favorite band, the Paramours. Teenage Belle had a secret crush on the lead singer. Tall with wavy dark hair, he reminded her of Lucky.

Lollygagging wouldn't get her any answers.

She used the stairway to the attic. Growing up, this was her place to escape. She'd play with discarded bows stacked neatly at the left side of the room and imagine every arrow hit their target. That didn't last long until she got bored.

Sometimes she'd don a scarlet cloak, snatch a picnic basket from the corner, and pretend to be Little Red Riding Hood. She'd stand in front of an oval mirror and act out the story. There would be no big bad wolf, only a friendly dog who became her pet. Other times, she'd become Snow White with seven lop eared bunnies that adored her.

One day, she had used her magic to create an imaginary

friend—a little boy who looked just like her. He would join her for tea, play with stuffed animals, or dress up in the clothing Belle found in an old chest. She had a special connection with this friend. He was the brother she had always longed for. She knew he wasn't real, although the idea of him brought her comfort. After she met Cami in grade school, they became best friends. That must have been when she stopped imagining the little boy.

She sat in an old rocker and scanned the room. The chest lay at her feet. Why not start there?

Pulling out a silky ball gown, she swirled her dust to try it on. Except for hitting her calves, it fit well. She wondered if this might have belonged to Zinnia. The matching leather slippers were way too tiny for her feet. She could use her magic to get them resized, but why bother? The satin slippers she wore were fine.

As she continued to sift through the chest, she kept eyeing the desk. Her intuition said to search it. She fit her hands in the slots and pushed the rollers up to the top. A quill pen attached to a glittery crimson feather next to a dried-up bottle of ink and a blotter. To the left, an envelope had been addressed to Rufus Brooks. Her great great grandfather lost their family's elite position because of a rumored affair with a mortal. After visiting Earth and enjoying her time with Lucky, Belle wondered if the affair were true.

That would be noteworthy information, even if it didn't tie to Aunt Zinnia.

She tried to tame her excitement as she carefully got out

the page. This could be the clue she'd been looking for. She read the note. An invitation to a ball held at Aphrodite's Castle.

Interesting—but not what she was looking for.

At the back of the desk sets of rectangular cubbies were empty. In the middle section were two rows with four miniature drawers on each side. She pulled each one out, starting on the right.

All four were empty.

She checked the left side. The second drawer contained a skeleton key.

The only drawer requiring a key was the long center one.

Belle's heart raced as she held the key and inserted it into the hole. Then her heart sunk.

An archery training manual. She looked through the pages. Nothing out of the ordinary.

Frigging thunderation! She needed a break.

Wait a minute. She'd recently watched a mystery movie where a drawer had a false bottom. She tapped on the wood. It sounded hollow, so she pressed on the right side corner. The opposite corner lifted slightly so she grasped it with her fingertips and pulled it off. Underneath, she spotted a scroll on two golden rods with heart-shaped tips.

It looked old.

She used her magical dust to lift it out and unroll pink linen paper from right to left in front of her. She recognized the Brook's Family Coat of Arms with the bubbling brook symbol adorning the center.

No doubt this belonged to her family.

Characters had been penned on both sides of the coat of arms. The fancy calligraphy wasn't Greek or French, but a language she couldn't decipher. Might be Arabic or Japanese. Running her pointer finger over the words, a spark of energy flowed through her. A sign that something significant would be found here. If only she could decipher the words.

Well, this scroll was hers now. She used her magic to roll it and send the scroll to her former bedroom. Once she'd secured the false bottom, set the archery guide on top, closed and locked the drawer, put the key in the proper place, and secured the top, she rushed back to her room and packed the scroll at the bottom of her bag. Another mystery to solve.

Would she ever get any answers?

The grandfather clock in the hallway chimed four times. She jumped. Taking a deep breath, she needed to chill. Her sister was meeting her for dinner in thirty minutes.

Checking her reflection in the mirror, she still wore the gown from the attic chest. With the flick of her fingertips, her magical dust swirled a pink knee-length dress around her body, and she headed out the door.

CHAPTER 15

Friday afternoon, Belle glanced around the office. In the conference room, three specialists used a virtual display at a corner table. Typically, she would have been curious about their project, but not today.

It was a good thing her boss was on vacation because she couldn't concentrate on work. Spending the weekend with her sister turned out to be enjoyable. They went out to dinner, took in a movie, and slept in late on Sunday.

Venecia had a date for the dance the following Saturday and asked Belle for advice on what to wear. They had tried on dozens of gowns while they chatted. Her sister's eyes lit whenever she talked about her boyfriend. She told Belle kissing him had been more exciting than riding a unicorn across a meadow.

Belle recalled her first kiss with Lucky. Holy smokes,

remembering the mortal's kiss made her hot even now. Venecia had noticed her blushing and asked if she was in love with Wynton. Belle said she wasn't sure. It was a bald-faced lie that made her feel awful, even though the lie might aid her future trips to Earth.

Belle shook off the guilt. The deception wouldn't have been necessary if her family hadn't been honest about Zinnia.

Frustration surged through her brain. She needed answers to a whole list of questions.

Who had hidden the scroll inside a false drawer in the attic? It must link to something important?

Had Zinnia been banished from Cupid's Corner or just from the Brooks family?

What were the facts?

Her aunt married a mortal. A black mark on the sainted Brooks family would make Grand Dame irate.

Why hadn't G-Dad stopped this nonsense?

She doubted Uncle Pete had been involved, not after he stuck up for Zinnia. Maybe a bigger question would be why had Zinnia's life history disappeared?

Hypothesizing wouldn't get her answers.

She'd brought over the Book of Relationships and clicked on Troy Anderson's file three times. Once again, a big X came up with the word corrupted. Dratted dragons!

Belle tapped her fingers on her desk.

Why won't it open? She swirled magical dust on the keyboard, pushed enter, chewed her lip and waited for the file. A folder labeled Troy Anderson-Personal Information appeared. She clicked on it. A full-size binder floated and dropped onto her desk. Flames appeared and burned the pages without any smoke. Charcoal like particles floated on top of her desk and spelled out:

B-E-W-A-R-E.

What in the universe was this?

She flicked her fingertips, allowing her magical dust to remove the warning, closed the program, and shut down her virtual computer by waving her hand.

My gosh, that was intense.

Four melodic chimes announced the end of the workday, and she was more than ready to visit Earth with Serenity later this evening.

She flew out of the office, headed outside, fluttered down the street, and floated to the ground inside her apartment's foyer. Outside Serenity's door, she knocked. Her friend should be back from her training by now. Time to tell Serenity her family's secret before they left for the world below.

"Hey," Serenity parted her cloud-covered door. "Come on in."

They both sat on the couch.

"How'd the training go?"

"A gryphon could pick up the new system better than those inputters I worked with. It's been a long week, but I'm ready for the weekend." Serenity wore an I-can't-wait-to party-grin.

"Me, too." Belle better mention Aunt Zinnia in case Lucky said something. The scroll could wait until later. "I need to tell you the real reason I went to Earth."

"Had a feeling there was more to your story," Serenity said.

"Have you ever heard of Zinnia Brooks?"

"Any relation to your dad?"

"She's his sister, my aunt. I overheard her name at a family dinner. She's been banished. Grand Dame refuses to allow anyone to talk about her."

"Wow! No wonder you've been acting a little nervous lately."

Belle hoped no one else noticed. "I've been trying to find info on her. There's nothing. Even in old photos, her image has been lifted."

"That's pretty extreme. Whoever did that *has* power."

"I know." Belle thought about the 'beware' message but decided not to say anything yet.

"Did you mention Zinnia to Lucky?"

"Yes. He took me to the address I found for her in Friendly City. She's moved, but I learned she married a Troy Anderson." Belle let out a disgruntled groan. "The last few weeks, I couldn't find anything about her or Troy in the Book of Relationships."

"Why didn't you ask for my help?"

Belle shrugged. "It's a sensitive family matter."

"I'll be happy to assist you." Serenity rubbed her hands together. "Looks like Monday we're solving a mystery."

"You're an awesome friend."

"I do my best." Serenity gave her a hug. "Can't wait to party on Earth. By the way, before we leave, you should create dark clothing so you'll blend in with the night.

"Good idea." Last visit, the invisibility potion hid what Belle wore. Too bad she'd use the rest of the potion for her ascent home. She shuddered at the thought of getting caught.

"I'm gonna catch a nap so I can be up all night."

"See you at ten." Belle fluttered above the curved staircase to her second-floor apartment, used her dust to part the cloud-covered door, and dropped into her favorite chair with the daisy-print covering. Cupids tended to go for shades of red, pink, and white, with an occasional blue tossed in. Belle created this chair with daisies as a silent act of rebellion.

She called, "Claire, show me casual dark-colored outfits women wear on Earth."

A flat page with about a hundred options floated in front of her. Tapping on the woman wearing indigo skinny jeans, a long top, and a waist-length jacket, she twirled her fingers to have the model turn around. "Replace my gown with this outfit." She flicked her fingertips and the human clothing formed around her body.

I HAVE to see what I look like.

. . .

Walking into her bedroom, she admired her Earthly style in the oval mirror. The jeans might be a bit stiff but fit great. The lace-up boots with tall heels gave her a biker chick appearance. Funny how she'd always been self-conscious about her height here in Cupid's Corner, but not on Earth.

Would Lucky like it? Her heart pitter-pattered. She wondered if he'd live up to the piquant illusion in her daydreams. The quick trip meant she only needed outfits for Saturday and Sunday. Not sure whether to pick another pair of jeans, shorts and a blouse or a short navy dress, she chose everything, along with high heels and tennis shoes. She floated her clothing and folded the items neatly inside her backpack.

Now for filling those extra vials of magic. She shuddered to think what would have happened if the vials she'd tucked in her backpack had been stolen during her last visit. In essence, without the magical dust, she could be trapped on Earth in human form with no means to return home.

With one still full, she filled three others with silvery-violet dust from her fingertips, capped them, and zipped two in a pocket inside her backpack.

Since she and Serenity would be staying in a hotel, a purse would come in handy when they were out. She looked at black purses, chose a Coach shoulder bag with a silver chain, and slipped the other two vials in a zippered pocket.

Serenity said twenties were easiest to spend. Belle flicked her fingertips and created two bundles, each worth three hundred dollars. She placed one bundle in her backpack, the second inside the purse. Adding snacks from her kitchen, Belle's pulse sped. She couldn't wait to be on that exciting planet.

With hours to kill, she pulled down a box in her closet, set it on her bed, and sifted through it. A tennis racket, porcelain doll, silver baby spoon, high school sweatshirt, and a stuffed unicorn. "Uni," she inspected her childhood toy. Its white wings drooped. Its rainbow mane looked a bit ratty, but as she held it close to her chest, a sense of calm filled her spirit. It connected her to a missing part from deep in her soul. Weird.

She glanced at the clock. Six minutes past eight. Might as well watch a show and pick up on some Earthly customs. "Claire, list TV comedies in the United States."

The Big Bang Theory.

Not interested.

The Bachelor.

The concept of a male dating twenty-five females held no appeal.

Heartland.

The blurb said it's about relationships on a ranch in

Canada. Her roommate fell in love with the rancher. This show might give Belle insight into her friend's new life.

"Play *Heartland*," she said.

The main character had a gift for working with horses. The horse's temperament varied, similar to the unicorns she'd rented from Aphrodite's Stables. The location reminded her of Calypso Forest if it had pine trees rather than flowering wisteria and redwoods. Enthralled with the beautiful scenery and the daily drama on the ranch, the doorbell chimed.

"Ten already," Belle set Uni on the coffee table and yawned as she parted the cloud door.

Serenity dyed her strawberry blonde hair an ebony shade and colored her wings black. She wore black leather pants and a long-sleeved black leather jacket that clung to her body. Only her face and hands remained a peachy tone. "You planning to marry Hades?"

"I could say the same for you. Love the boots."

"Thanks. How many vials of magical dust are you bringing?" Belle asked.

"Four. One will usually suffice for reentry home as long as the wind doesn't kick in and spread it across the land. I learned to change into my Cupid shape inside an Earthly building before returning."

"You never said how many times you've visited Earth." Belle was curious.

"Close to thirty." Serenity tilted her head. "Cute purse.

Looks a lot like mine." She held up a smaller purse with a braided handle. "How much money are you bringing?"

"Six hundred, all twenties."

"I brought the same. What address did you use on your ID?"

"Never thought of bringing one." Belle hadn't needed an ID before. "I told Lucky the standard location, I live in Heavenly Valley."

"The address for the Celestial Apartments on Celestial Avenue in Heavenly is on my license." Serenity swirled her coppery dust. A driver's license floated into Belle's hand. She looked inside her purse and pulled out a plastic Visa card. "Take this thousand-dollar pre-paid debit card, just in case."

"You've thought of everything." Her friend's ingenuity amazed Belle.

"I try. Now, lead us on to your handsome human."

"I still want to take time to search for my aunt while I'm there."

"Maybe Lucky will have a lead." Serenity folded her arms. "The hotel might have computer access. Otherwise, let's enjoy ourselves. First thing Monday, I'll start digging."

Belle propped open the window and flew out. Serenity followed. They passed the next apartment building to the north. Lights flickered inside various rooms. Symphony music intermingled with rock and roll.

A trio of teenagers flew on the other side of the street. "Flutter faster Zelda," one of the girls yelled. "Can't be the last ones at the party." They zipped off.

Turning east into the Calypso Forest, Belle and Serenity didn't talk, not about to draw attention to themselves. The bright moon gave off plenty of light. It would be full when they headed back on Monday. At least they wouldn't have to rely on the last light of a sunbeam and chance running into a Cupid guard at the top.

They passed the first moonbeam near the Fates River. "Is this the one you took?" Serenity asked.

"No. It's between two redwood trees." Belle said. Some fifty yards further, they found the spot.

"Make yourself human size here. That way you won't have to use your vial to change when you land."

If Belle had done that before her last descent, it would have saved her a lot of aggravation. Still, she couldn't figure out why she'd transformed into a naked human when she hadn't used any magic. She shrugged, flicked her fingertips and swirled her silvery-purple dust around herself. In less than a second, Belle's clothing grew with her as she became a tenth as big as one of the redwoods.

Belle wrapped her arms around a luminescent column and descended toward the Northern Hemisphere.

She heard Serenity count, "One Aphrodite, two Aphrodites, three Aphrodites," and joined her on the moonbeam.

Belle sailed down toward the Northern Hemisphere a lot quicker as a human. "You're gonna have to jump a beam to the west," she called and jumped from one edge to the center of another.

"Got it." Serenity stayed on her tail.

Spotting the Colorado River, Belle yelled, "One more leap and we'll be in California." She sprung to the last beam and pretended she rode down a giant slide standing.

"Use your heels to slow your speed," Serenity yelled.

Putting her toes up and leaning slightly back, her speed slowed, and she landed smoothly on the grass in front of Tranquility Car Rentals.

"Let's get a car. I'll do the talking." Serenity smirked.

"Let me drive first, please." Driving a chariot, she had to deal with a winged Pegasus. How much harder would a car be?

"Sure. Hope we can get something sporty."

Minutes later, Serenity paid for the rental with a pre-paid Visa card, and they got into a Mustang convertible and buckled up.

Belle pressed the start button. "Why won't it do anything?"

"You have to have your foot on the break."

"That's dumb." But it vroomed.

"What's the address of the bar? I'll put it in."

Belle looked through her purse and handed her Lucky's card.

"It's only five miles which is good. It's nearly eleven. How late is that bar open?" Serenity asked.

"'Till two.

"Then let's get going. Take your foot off the brake. Before

you put the car in gear, try out the gas pedal and get a feel for it."

Belle revved the engine. "This motor sounds powerful."

"I think I should drive and let you learn by watching." Serenity squinted at her.

"Nope. I see the shifter is on the console. D is for drive, right?"

"It is."

The car accelerated quicker than Belle planned. When she got to the turn off for the street, she slammed on the brakes.

"Good thing I'm wearing my seatbelt."

"Quiet. I am getting the hang of this." She turned onto the road without any problem. "There aren't maybe people out."

Serenity was white-knuckling the sides of the seat.

Moonlight flickered off Tranquility Lake's water. Belle's lips tingled recalling her first mortal kiss.

The GPS announced the next turn in two miles.

"We'll pass the hotel first. Let's check in and refresh our makeup." Belle wanted to look her best for Lucky.

They sped east.

"Take your foot off the gas and slow down to forty. The last thing we need right now is to get pulled over."

"Where'd you learn to drive?"

"A gorgeous guy I met while snowboarding in Colorado taught me." Serenity laughed.

"Don't you ever worry about getting caught?"

"Not really. Cupid archer's frequently visited Earth. Why shouldn't we?"

"Because it's against the rules." Belle's pulse sped faster, and she hit the curb as she pulled into the hotel's parking lot. "Sorry."

"For a newbie driver, you're doing okay."

"Thanks." Belle planned to master this driving thing.

"Is this where you stayed?"

"No." She would've stayed there if her money hadn't been stolen.

"Another hotel nearby?"

"I stayed in Lucky's room."

"Really." Serenity lifted an eyebrow.

"It wasn't like that. I slept alone in his studio. He slept elsewhere." Still, she wasn't totally opposed to the idea.

CHAPTER 16

Lucky's new waitress called in sick, and the Rebel Rouser Tavern hopped. Shorthanded on a Friday night. Shit. Not again.

Folks were generally mellow but might get agitated if they waited too long for a drink. Unpredictable drunks sometimes got crazy. He broke up a brawl last Saturday. Two bull-headed men argued over who won at pool. His jaw still smarted from the left hook.

He served the first half of the ten-foot bar closest to the door, his partner handled the other end. With most tables filled, customers kept him busy shagging drinks. The two empty seats in front of him at the bar gave him access to scan the area. So far, nobody seemed rowdy. Four couples danced to "Leader of the Pack" in an area about as big as a patchwork quilt. More folks trickled in through the front door.

Lucky removed empty glasses, wiped off the top of the bar, and glanced toward the door to his left. "Crazy Little Thing Called Love" came on. The song reminded him of that night Belle sauntered up to him with a drink order. "Have you ever been crazy in love?" she'd asked. Her violet eyes shone with curiosity. He hadn't bothered answering.

Love never lasted.

Dating his share of beautiful women, no one captured his complete attention until Belle charged into his life. A temporary diversion. If only his thoughts would quit swinging back to her.

A baseball game played on the giant flat-screen TV directly across from the bar. He watched a player hit one over the fence past center field. "Yes! That's it," he said to his friend, Havoc, sitting on the barstool in front of Lucky. Others in the bar cheered.

"It's Griswald's tenth grand slam for the season." Ace held up his mug to tribute the player.

At a table not far from the restrooms toward the back of the saloon, two burly men arm wrestled. "You cheated," one of the men shouted. The other cocked his fist back.

Instinct had Lucky ready to jump over the bar, but Geezer was a few feet closer, and shouted, "Knock it off."

The men glared at each other. One got up and left in a huff.

Yep, this was gonna be one of those nights.

A chick in a red dress walked in. He thought it might be

Belle, but as the woman stepped closer, he noticed blonde hair.

"You okay," Havoc asked.

"Yep." Why couldn't he quit thinking about Belle? Whenever he picked up a wrench in his garage, he imagined her next to him. Yesterday, a friend came to the house to figure out why his taillight didn't work. Using a manual, he tracked down a short. Belle would've liked solving this problem.

Havoc held up his hand for another beer.

"Where's Thorny tonight?" Lucky slid a new draft in front of his friend.

"His grandfather died."

That comment punched at Lucky's gut, reminding him of his own grandfather's passing.

A bearded guy ordered four longnecks and brought them to friends at a table. Others came up. He poured more drafts, a couple of mixed drinks, and filled bowls with peanuts.

"Hey, Lucky. Havoc." That voice belonged to Belle

Lucky couldn't hide his grin as he glanced at her.

"This is Serenity." Belle stripped off her dark jacket, revealing a sleeveless blouse. Soft. Feminine. He glanced at her black-haired friend. Stunning, but she wasn't Belle.

Serenity flashed Belle a thumbs up. "Whoa, girl. You've been keeping some secrets from me."

Belle ignored her friend and gave him a wink.

"What'll it be, ladies?" he asked.

"Sex on the Beach," Belle said in a low sensual tone.

Images of her gorgeous body, dripping wet in a swimsuit, made his lower extremities twitch.

"I want that." Serenity's black leather pants shimmied as she moved to the other side of Havoc and took the empty barstool. No surprise. His friend attracted women like bees to honey.

"Put their drinks on my tab." Havoc shifted to face Serenity.

"Thanks." Both girls said in unison.

His friend removed the cap he'd worn backward and combed his fingers through his hair. "Name's Havoc."

"Makes me think of trouble."

Havoc shrugged. "You like trouble?"

"On occasion," Serenity rubbed her hand on his knee and spread her fingers.

Lucky could practically feel sparks shooting between those two. He added peach schnapps, vodka, orange, and cranberry juice into a shaker, poured the drinks and set one in front of each woman.

Serenity sipped her drink. "This is scrumptious."

"It sure is." Belle licked her lips, the same pedal-soft lips he'd kissed.

Focus. Concentrate on something else. A customer closest to the door motioned for another draft, which he poured.

"What brings you to town?" Havoc asked.

"Belle's description of this bar, her ride to the lake, and

the handsome man she'd stayed with. Had to see this place for myself."

"You said I was handsome?" he whispered to her, a ridiculous thrill pulsed through him.

"Maybe." She lifted a shoulder.

"Did she tell you how they met?" Havoc rested his hand on the back of Serenity's chair.

"No."

"She broke a booze bottle in his stockroom. Lucky picked her up, tossed her over his shoulder, and hauled her out of here."

Lucky's face got warm, his irritation at his friend, blazing. "Thought Belle came in to steal some liquor." He glanced at Belle. "You never said why you were there."

"I needed to adjust my dress and your women's bathroom was occupied." She twirled the straw around and around her drink.

"Guess I overreacted, but I did apologize later."

"You more than made up for it." She smiled, and his pulse sped faster. Crazy.

"Where are you ladies staying?" Havoc asked.

"Checked into the Tranquility Hotel. After being on the road for hours, it felt great to walk the few blocks here." Serenity placed her hand on Havoc's shoulder. "I'm all for fresh air."

"You take the bus?" Lucky asked.

"Not today," Belle said. "Serenity rented a Mustang."

"Love fast cars. Besides my Harley, I've got a Hellcat Challenger."

"Impressive." Serenity leaned a little closer.

"Wanna help me pick out a couple songs on the jukebox?" Havoc stood and offered his hand. "You can tell me about your ride while we dance."

"Sure."

The two weaved their way toward the front door, leaving Belle by Lucky. "Born to Be Wild" played. "Belle," her name rolled off his tongue. "Any news on your aunt?"

"Nothing." She sipped her drink. "It's frustrating."

"I bet. Gran has a friend who's into genealogy. She'll be in town on Monday. Think you'll be around?"

"No. We leave Sunday afternoon."

"Well, I've got the next two days here." Her sultry voice made his pulse sped up a little.

"Got any specific plans?"

"Just to come here. Other than that, who knows?"

Several couples slow danced to a twangy country western song, one of the couples included Havoc and Serenity. "Looks like your friend's enjoying herself."

"Serenity thinks of life as a party. She's fun to hang with."

"As I recall, so are you."

That made her blush. Serenity came back and dragged her over to the floor for a line dance.

Havoc took his seat and motioned for another beer. "Serenity's hot."

"And lively I see."

"Nothing wrong with that." Havoc turned to watch her dance.

A guy at the bar waved for beers for him and his girlfriend. Lucky turned and waited on them and a few more customers.

"The ladies picked a busy weekend with the carnival tomorrow," Havoc said.

"It's for a good cause. Being a foster kid can be tough." Lucky knew first hand how hard it could be.

"What booth are you stuck with?"

"Cotton candy." It was a sticky booth but not that bad.

"Sweet." Havoc chuckled and went to find Serenity.

Belle came back flushed from dancing. "That was invigorating."

"You're quite a dancer." Lucky noticed how her hips swiveled. Damn seductive. "You take classes."

"Ballet and tap. Always wanted to try jazz."

"Bet you'd be good. You seem to excel at everything." He set another drink in front of her.

"You're a nice guy."

"Shh. Don't want that getting around." He helped another customer.

When he turned back toward her, Serenity stood behind Belle. "Mind if I go for a ride with Havoc?"

"Not at all."

"I'll pay for your Uber to the hotel," Serenity offered.

"No need. I'll be more than happy to drop her off." If he

knew anything about Havoc, the cute little spitfire wouldn't be returning to her room tonight.

"See you later." Her friend met Havoc at the door.

Ten more people came in, filling the last two tables in the bar. He could use the help. "Wanna make extra cash."

"Definitely." Her eyes glimmered.

He grabbed the caddy he'd already fixed for the no-show waitress. "Go ahead and get their orders."

She fit right in wearing all black, including those knee-high lace-up boots. "I Won't Back Down" blared from the jukebox. Belle grinned as she marched towards him. "That's your song."

"Hell yeah." The fact that she remembered amazed hit a soft spot. He wouldn't mind having her alone and see where it leads. He couldn't wait until closing, hoping to take this intriguing woman back to his place.

CHAPTER 17

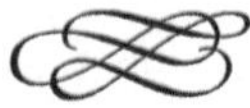

Belle got a kick out of conversing with people as she waited on tables.

"Found my Panhead in a barn in Kansas," an older guy said.

"Do the cylinder heads really look like cake pans?" Belle had read that in one of Lucky's magazines.

"Sure do. You own a bike, missy?" A younger man eyed her from top to bottom. Not handsome, he had a kind face. As long as he didn't touch her, she was okay with him looking.

"Not yet." Thinking about riding with Lucky, she glanced in his direction, and he winked at her. What a flirt.

The old-timer motioned to the bar. "Lucky should be able to fix you up when you're ready."

"Good to know," she said politely and cleared glasses

from an empty table to her right. Driving her own motorcycle next to Lucky, she'd probably be watching him instead of where she was going. For now, it'd be safer riding with him.

She walked toward the station and handed him her order.

"You doing okay out there?"

"Splendid."

He flashed her one of his incredible smiles with those darn dimples. Serenity wasn't wrong when she called him hunky. Belle fanned her face with her hand. Holy Aphrodite, this guy could make a snowman melt.

"It is rather stuffy in here," he said. "Guess I should turn up the A.C."

"I'll survive."

"Leader of the Pack" played. The music made the sound of a motorcycle revving. She thought about how Lucky seemed to rev up her passion for adventure. Comparing him to the Cupid males she'd dated was like comparing a fireworks finale with a sparkler.

Several minutes later, Lucky shouted, "Last call."

The night had flown by.

The clientele had thinned, and now only two tables were occupied. She took their orders and went up to Lucky. "Five drafts and two screwdrivers."

The intensity in his gaze made her heart beat faster.

He filled her orders; she stared at his dexterous hands. Strong hands that could easily loosen nuts and bolts.

"Once you settle the tabs, total up your sales in the office." His deep voice sent tingles along her spine.

"Yes, sir." She saluted, teasing him for commanding her.

"What if I said, please?"

"Too little too late." She grabbed her tray and steadied it on the palm of her hand.

"You're impossible, princess."

No longer finding the nickname irritating, she added an extra swing in her hips, confident he'd be watching. It didn't take long to deliver the drinks and collect on the tabs.

Waving at Lucky, she headed into the office. The wall clock above the desk read 1:47 a.m. Totaling the receipts with the printing calculator she'd used last time, adrenaline buzzed inside her from the glorious night. She stood to head back into the bar.

The door whooshed open, and she sensed Lucky standing behind her. "How'd you do?"

"Twenty-seven dollars."

"Take an extra twenty for wages." He set the cash register drawer on the desk, bundled up the money into a pouch, added a deposit slip on the top, and pulled back a framed James Dean poster on the wall. "Now you know all my secrets," he said as he placed the cash into the safe, shut it, and swung the picture in place.

"I highly doubt that."

"You're too much." His arm slipped around her shoulders, and she found herself pinned against the door. His lips crushed against hers, and he deepened the kiss, enflaming her mouth. His hard body pressed against her. Heck, her whole body warmed.

He pulled away. "Been dying to do that all night."

Her legs were wobbly, but she managed to step back. The door opened with Lucky's partner. "You're still here." He wore a know-what-you-two-were-doing grin.

Her hand flew to her lips as if covering them could hide the evidence of their kiss.

"We were just leaving." He reached on the shelf behind him, handed her a helmet, clasped her hand, and ushered her outside. "You're cute when you blush."

"Think so." Holy Zeus, she liked how he said *cute*.

"Yep." They reached his bike out front.

She glanced over to the bench on the north side of the dirt lot, recalling how livid she'd been when he'd carried her out back. My how things had changed.

"You're staying at the hotel up the street, right?"

She gazed at him, the streetlight illuminating his strong chin with a midnight shadow.

"The hotel?"

She'd been caught gawking. "It's up this street."

"Good. Have any plans for tomorrow?" He hopped onto his Harley.

She wrapped her arms around his waist. "I might go to the lake with Serenity."

"Havoc and I are helping at a carnival. If you ladies are free, stop by the cotton candy booth. My shift starts at noon. After I finish, we can go for a ride."

Butterflies fluttered inside. "Are you asking me out?"

"If you're interested," he said, his voice low.

They took off. The now familiar rumble and vibrations of the engine awakened an inner euphoria. She loved riding with him. He parked his motorcycle and got off, as did she. "I'll walk you to the lobby."

"Sure."

He held her hand.

"How's that Sportster coming along?"

"The engine's fixed. Could use an extra set of hands with other things if there's time."

"Maybe Sunday morning?"

"I'd like that." He held the door for her.

"Thanks for bringing me here." She yawned.

"It's late." He bent down and pressed his lips to her cheek.

Disappointed in that chaste caress, she thought about pulling him back, but since they were at the front entrance, she nixed the idea.

"Hope to see you tomorrow. Call if you need a ride." And he was gone.

She strolled past a silver-haired clerk with thick glasses reading a romance novel, rode the elevator to the second floor, veered right, held the card key in front of the door, switched on the lights, and glanced at the beds.

Empty.

Serenity was still out with Havoc.

Wound up, she could use a stiff drink. She peered inside the mini-fridge under the sink.

Whiskey? Nope.

Vodka? Maybe with orange juice.

Chardonnay. Perfect. The top twisted off. She poured the wine into a glass, lounged in one of the orange chairs next to a table, and drank. "Ah, this is the life."

"What is?" Serenity asked.

"There's white wine in the fridge. Unless you'd rather help yourself to whiskey?"

"Wine works."

"Did you enjoy your moonlit ride?"

"It was marvelous. I'm in love."

Belle curled her lips.

"This time I mean it. He led me to a hilltop overlooking Tranquility Lake, told me I'm the most beautiful woman he'd ever seen, and when he kissed me, I swear, fireworks exploded." Serenity held up her glass. "To kissing humans."

"Oh, yes." A snort slipped out.

"Might sleep with him tomorrow night," Serenity said as nonchalantly as if she were picking out a new shade of fingernail polish.

Belle choked, grabbed a bottle of water off the counter and downed it. "I'm not sure that's wise?"

"Don't tell me you haven't thought about sex with Lucky."

"Maybe." The heated kiss in his office fired her desire. "But doubt I'll go through with it."

"Why not? You already know he's a hunk." Serenity waved a finger at her.

"He's a human."

"I get that you're cautious." Serenity crossed her legs. "But—"

"I originally snuck down here to find my aunt. I consider that pretty adventurous."

"And you weren't sent to Hades Harem?"

"Because I wasn't caught." She couldn't help shivering at the thought of being sent to that realm supposedly near the core of Earth.

"You do realize Hades doesn't have a harem. It's one of those old tales told to keep us in line."

"I know. It's hard to let go of the taboos ingrained in me. You know—Cupid guilt."

"As far as guilt," Serenity frowned. "I gave it up ages ago."

"How'd you do it?" Belle met her friend a few years after she left her hometown of Lover's Landing.

"After my parents disowned me because I gave up shooting, they thought I'd never make it on my own doing anything else. But I've showed them."

"You sure did. Plus, Cami and I gained a wonderful friend in the process."

"Back at you." Serenity finished her wine and yawned. "It's getting late. Promised Havoc I'd stop by his booth tomorrow."

"Told Lucky the same." Out of habit, Belle flicked her fingertips, and silvery-purple dust swirled a short nightie around her body.

"Please don't use your magic here," Serenity squeaked. "Archers combine their magical dust with the potion added to an arrow. When the arrow connects with a mortal on Earth, a computer in Cupid's Corner can track the dust."

"So that's how the council found Cami's error."

"It is, although it has plenty of glitches. Since we don't shoot arrows, I'm not too concerned right now, but I'd rather be cautious. A prototype that tracks all magical activity on Earth is being developed. At least, it's not up and running yet." Serenity let out a relieved breath.

"Now look who's being prudent." She ran her fingertips over the emblem to mask the effects.

"I happen to like sneaking to Earth." Serenity puffed up her pillow.

The secrecy behind her aunt forced Belle's adventurous side to come out. Now, she was wild about this planet. "I wonder if my aunt fell in love with this wondrous place and chose to stay."

"No doubt." Serenity switched off her light. "We can talk more tomorrow. I need my beauty sleep."

CHAPTER 18

At a quarter to noon on Saturday, Lucky pulled into a space at the Tranquility Community Park right behind Havoc's brand-new dresser. The bike, designed for comfort, had a windshield, plush seats, and extra-large saddlebags. Lucky preferred the simplicity of his Knucklehead.

"Think the ladies will show today?" Havoc asked as he put down his kickstand.

"Probably." Lucky shrugged.

A carnival banner on the fencepost led them to the entrance. They walked along a sidewalk toward the ticket booth with a long line of people that reached the grassy center of the park. Past them, dozens of red-and-white booths were set up on both sides.

"You and Serenity seemed to hit it off."

"She's different."

Lucky didn't pry, figuring whatever went on with those two was none of his business. They veered to the right behind the booths, past the people blowing up balloons and tacking them to a board for a dart game, and by a couple setting out small bowls for ping-pong goldfish.

"This is me." Havoc stepped over PVC piping and into the spin art booth.

"Enjoy yourself."

"I plan to. Wanna meet by the concession stands about two?" his friend asked.

"Sure." Lucky continued on, past the hot dog stand to the cotton candy booth. Directions were taped on the table next to the cylinder.

"Could you use an assistant?"

He looked up and saw Belle. "You bet."

She shimmied over the booth's PVC piped construction on the side. In a form-fitting yellow tank top, her full breasts filled it out. He tried to ignore his growing attraction but found it nearly impossible with her wearing Daisy Duke shorts.

"You ever make cotton candy?"

"I've eaten plenty. Does that count?" She laughed.

"Not really." He took her hand and pulled her toward the machine.

"How's it work?"

Not many women would care about the technical end.

One of the reasons he liked being around her. “It blows hot air and swirls the heated sugar?”

She gave him a wry grin and tossed her braid over her shoulder.

He wouldn’t mind unraveling the braid and running his fingers through her wavy hair. He sucked in his breath. Now was not the time. “Should we start with pink or blue?” He held up two cylinder-shaped containers.

“Pink.” She snatched the sugar floss from his hand.

“You’re such a girl.” He couldn’t resist teasing. “Anyway, we fill the floss head with about a cup.” Flipping the switch, the machine roared. The sugary aroma mixed with fried corn dogs from the next booth over. He dipped a stick into the candy and set the end of the fluffy result into a wooden holder. “You try.”

She pulled off one of the stacked paper sticks.

“Hold the pointed end between two fingers and your thumb and wind the sugary mess around it.”

He watched her maneuver the stuff.

“Is this your first experience running this booth?”

“Hardly. My foster parents used to run it.” He dipped another stick into the machine and set it in the holder.

She eyed him sideways. “You were in a foster home? I’ve heard about such an arrangement but never knew anyone that was placed in one. What happened?”

“I told you my mom ran off with her boss.” He swirled two wands. His gut tied up in knots. “By the time I turned eleven, he was out of control. Then came a DUI. CPS found us home alone and brought us to some stranger's place."

"Why didn't Gran take you?"

"She and Gramps had been in Arizona helping out his father after a stroke. When she called to check on us, and I didn't answer, she knew something had happened and came back. It took about six months for my grandparents to gain custody of us." His sister didn't understand why they were living with strangers. Thankfully, Gran called often, although she wasn't allowed to visit either of them while she filled out tons of paperwork and dealt with social workers.

"I'm sorry." She set her hand on his arm.

"No reason to be. I'm fine." No sense dwelling on the past, he filled the floss container again and heard voices. A mother with a young child waited at the front of the booth. "We've got customers. You mind making the cones while I help them?"

"Not at all."

He handed a little boy the spun sugar; his eyes were as wide as saucers.

Lucky turned back to Belle. She made four lopsided balls and must've wiped her hand to her forehead. A five-inch pink puff stuck straight up like a flamingo's feather. He couldn't help laughing.

"What's so funny?"

"This." He leaned over close enough that she could smell his masculine scent and pulled the candy off.

"I was saving that for later."

"Not anymore." He threw the puff in the trash. "I'll buy you some later."

"Hey, coach." Three boys from his swim team waved.

"Is that your girlfriend?" One teen asked.

"Just a friend."

Belle waved at them.

"Come over here and meet three rascals from my water polo team." He introduced them.

"It's a pleasure to meet you." She placed the candy in its holder.

"Hope to see you around." The teen left with his friends.

About ten people formed a line.

"Let's switch. Five tickets for each one."

"Sure."

He tried not to stare at her legs as she ambled in front of him but couldn't miss how long and well toned, they appeared. If they were alone, well—they weren't. He turned to the machine, adding more floss, dipping in one wand, and then another.

She reached for a candy order, and their fingertips touched.

A jolt of heat slammed right through his heart. "Did you feel that?"

"What?"

His imagination must be going wild. "Nothing."

They worked as a team, and the afternoon disappeared. He owed her an expensive dinner for lending a hand.

A middle-aged couple came for their shift. Lucky

showed them what to do and left with Belle. “Mind if we stop by Serenity and Havoc's booth and see if they're still there?”

“Not at all.” He grabbed her hand, dodged around a group of teens shooting darts at balloons, scurried past the people lined up for goldfish ping-pong, and stopped at the spin art table.

“This isn't face painting,” he said to Havoc who displayed long streaks of red and blue across his cheek.

“She keeps distracting me.” Havoc said, grinning at Serenity.

She picked up a bottle of yellow paint and splattered a blob onto his apron.

“Hey.”

Serenity smirked.

“You're wacky,” Belle said to her friend.

“Is she always so wild?” Havoc asked as he got a cloth and wiped off his face and apron.

“Always.”

Serenity assisted a little girl squirting paint onto the paper in the spinning machine. Havoc's gaze riveted to her.

“Sorry we're late.” A woman came in from the back followed by her two teenage daughters.

“No prob,” Havoc said, removing his apron. Serenity did the same.

“I'm starving. Thinking about getting a dog and fries,” Lucky said looping his arm around Belle. “How's that sound?”

"Make mine deep-fried grilled cheese." She flashed a smile at him. "If that's okay?"

"Whatever you want, princess."

"In that case, I'll take a Harley and riding lessons." She kissed his cheek.

"Once I finish that Sportster, I might consider it."

"THREE-LEGGED RACE STARTS IN TEN MINUTES." Someone announced over a speaker. "Grab your partner and head over to the stage area."

"What's that?" Belle asked.

"You and a partner tie your legs together to race. You game?"

Holy smokes, he gazed at her like she were a goddess. "You'd better be fast 'cause I aim to win." She couldn't resist saying.

"Not if we beat you to the finish line," Serenity said.

"Losing couple buys dinner tonight. And the two of us together can't lose." Havoc's arm went around Serenity's waist. The attraction between them singed the air.

"I'll let Belle decide if we go for American or Italian cuisine." Lucky's confidence in her ability was unwarranted.

"You're delusional. Serenity gets to choose."

They ambled to the south near the stage, dodging between a crowd forming along the perimeter to watch the race.

At least thirty contestants stood behind a chalked white line on the grass. A young guy wearing a bright yellow Hawaiian shirt and a goofy straw hat gave Lucky a long strip of material. Lucky leaned down and tied their ankles together. His hand grazed her thigh as he stood and put his arm around her waist. The closeness caused her body temperature to rise.

"Start running with your outside leg. Make sure your steps are in sync with mine." His warm breath caressed her skin.

"Got it," she said hoping she could concentrate on her task instead of the gorgeous guy next to her. "Can't wait to leave Serenity and Havoc in the dust."

Lucky chuckled. "We race on grass."

"It's a figurative image of our victory."

The man on the right of Belle asked his young daughter. "You sure you're up to this?" Coming to about Belle's elbow, the little girl didn't look any older than four or five.

"Yes, daddy. Mommy's watching us from the clouds."

Her mom must be a Cupid. How sad for them to be separated.

"The rules are simple, no pushing or shoving or cheating," a man holding a megaphone said. "Both feet behind the line. When I blow the whistle, the first one to make it to the other side wins."

"You're toast," Havoc said.

"You wish," Lucky chided back and pulled Belle closer.

"On your mark. Get set." The whistle sounded, and they were moving.

"We've got this," Lucky whispered. Then the little girl fell in front of him, forcing him to stop and knock Belle's stride off balance. She tumbled backward, landing on the ground as he assisted the little girl.

What a sweet gesture.

"Help me up." She couldn't stop laughing. "We're gonna lose."

He offered his hand to aide her, but she ended up pulling him to the grass next to her.

He kissed her quick on the lips. "Get up. We need to finish."

They tried to stand together and toppled down.

"We're pathetic." With Lucky at her side, she didn't mind one bit.

LUCKY AND BELLE reached the finish line dead last.

"Here you go." A man handed each of them a green participation ribbon. "Saw you helping out that little girl."

"Anyone would've done the same."

Havoc and Serenity waited off to the side at a bench. His arm looped around her.

"Guess dinner's on me," Lucky said.

"We'll go Dutch. Serenity and I were second."

"Can't believe we got beat by a silver-haired couple."

Serenity motioned to the smiling older people standing near the sidewalk and holding up a trophy.

"At least you weren't last."

Havoc's phone beeped. He glanced at the message. "Did you sign me up for the dunking booth?"

"It's for a good cause." Lucky held Belle's hand. "You any good at throwing a baseball."

"Got a mean curve."

"I don't doubt that. Be easy on me." His leg ached from that fall. Holding her hand, he weaved Belle through the throngs of people now filling the walkways.

"Never seen a dunking tank. How does it work?"

"Dunk tank," he corrected. "Watch. I'm guessing you'll figure it out pretty quickly." He pulled her toward a boxy container with a cage around the top. A woman threw a ball at the red target. The bottom dropped, and the guy toppled into the water. Water splashed as the high school soccer coach pulled himself onto the bench.

"You wanna take my place?" Lucky's hand went on her shoulder.

"Nope." She stepped back.

"Just asked Serenity the same thing." Havoc stepped beside him. "I think she'd look cute up there."

"Wet T-shirts aren't exactly family entertainment." Serenity stood next to Belle.

"Suppose you're right." Lucky could see parents complaining. "Guess I'd better go relieve Steve before he gets too waterlogged." He stripped off his shirt.

Catching Belle staring at his chest, he flexed his pecs. Then he unbuckled his belt and heard her gasp.

"Relax, I've got on swim trunks." He stuffed his shirt and pants inside his backpack, handed it to her, scooted up the metal ladder, opened the door into the tank, and positioned himself in the middle of a bench.

"Aim for the center of the bullseye, miss," the man running the booth said.

Belle held a baseball in her hand, wound up, and the ball nicked the edge.

"You can do it, Belle," her friend called from behind her.

She threw again, hit the center, and he tumbled into the water. He sputtered, coughed, and pulled himself back up onto the bench. "Two more dunks, and it's your turn, Havoc."

"To think we could've slipped away, babe," he said to Serenity.

"And miss seeing you wet and on display. Not on your life."

"I like your friend," Lucky whispered to Belle.

A woman he'd seen around town went next. All three attempts missed.

"Hey, coach." A teen held three baseballs. "Since your girlfriend's watching you, I'll go easy."

"I doubt that." If anything, the boy would show off for his friends.

Thwack. The ball hit the wall behind the tank.

Thwack. It skidded near the lever and bounced against the wall.

The teen wound up his arm, the ball sped for the center, and Lucky dropped into the tank. He jumped back on the bench.

"Ready to meet your maker, Lucky," Havoc tossed a ball to Serenity.

"Sure. One more dunk, and it's your turn." Lucky couldn't wait to get out of that tank.

As Belle watched him, she ran her tongue along the top of her lip. Either it was habit or seeing him shirtless was making her hot for him. He hoped the later.

Serenity aimed, hit the mark, and toppled him into the water.

CHAPTER 19

Seven-thirteen p.m.

After the carnival, Serenity drove back to the hotel, Belle showered and dressed in jeans and an off the shoulder pink eyelet blouse. Subtle but alluring.

In the bathroom, Serenity plastered her hair with hairspray.

"The helmet's gonna mess up all that work," Belle called to her friend.

"No, it won't." Serenity sprayed another layer onto her curled long bob. "Wish I was gifted with wavy hair like you."

"And I wanted straight blonde." Belle glanced at the clock on the nightstand. "Hurry up. We're already late."

"It's good to keep men waiting." Serenity came out

wearing black jeans and a low-cut cardinal red blouse. "Makes our entrance that much grander."

"You're wacky." Belle snatched her purse off the dresser.

"You look incredible." Serenity said as they rode the elevator down.

"As usual, you're a siren." Belle wished she were petite like her friend.

"I refuse to sing to lure Havoc's attention."

"Won't need to in that outfit," Belle said as they continued through to the lobby. "Besides, he's already interested in you."

Lucky and Havoc waited in chairs near a fireplace. Each man stood, but her focus was on Lucky. Her handsome rebel had shaved off his five o'clock shadow, wore dark denim jeans, a navy button-down shirt, and a smile that said he was happy to see her. "Hey, princess." He handed her a single burgundy-colored tulip. "Reminded me of you."

Her heart beat faster than a hummingbird's wings as she tucked the flower behind her ear. "Thanks."

"I'm starving. You ladies up for Italian?" Havoc asked with his arm around Serenity.

"Sounds divine." Serenity practically simpered.

"You clean up well," Lucky whispered in her ear. His warm breath caused goosebumps on her neck.

"Used the hose out back."

"Of course you did, my little country girl." He held her hand and brought her to his bike.

She got on the back, her head spinning fast. The motor

hummed. She adored riding with Lucky. On Earth, there were no Cupid rules to follow. No small community ready to gossip.

Cupids believed love could hit in an instant. Could that fluttery feeling whenever Lucky gazed at her be love? A ridiculous notion since she barely knew the man. Anyway, she didn't believe true love was her destiny.

They rode along the main boulevard for several blocks passing a bank and some strip malls. The lights from a car coming in the opposite direction shone directly into her eyes. She blinked to clear her focus.

Havoc's motorcycle pulled off to the right. Old Italy flashed in bright yellow. Lucky followed, parking next to Havoc at the side of the rectangular building.

Italian music played from the speakers. They were seated at a booth close to the bar. With her on the inside, Lucky scooted in so close their thighs touched. His arm reached along the back of the bench as if he were claiming her. Funny how when Wynton had done the same thing, it felt possessive and wrong. With Lucky, it felt right.

The hostess handed them menus.

A waiter offered two bottles of wine. "Would you care for Zinfandel or Chianti? The first bottle comes with the meal."

"What's Chianti?" Belle asked.

"It's a bold red flavor that goes well with pasta."

Lucky looked at Belle. "It's lady's choice."

"Chianti." Serenity chimed.

"Perfect." The waiter used his corkscrew to remove the cork and poured wine into the glasses on the table.

Belle took a sip. "This is good."

"Would you like to start with an appetizer of baked clams or braised meatballs?"

"Yuck," Serenity said what Belle thought.

"That's a—no," Havoc smirked. "Give us a minute to look over the menu."

The waiter left.

"I'm guessing you'd prefer to skip the meal and go for tiramisu or crème brûlée," Lucky's whisper tickled her ear.

"I'll save room for dessert. Right now, I'm debating over the fettuccini Alfredo or three-cheese ravioli."

"Let's get both and share," he said in a scrumptious sultry tone.

"Sure." She emptied her wine glass.

"How can you eat a poor defenseless bird?" Serenity wagged a finger at Havoc.

His mouth opened to retort, but then he shut it. Serenity had a valid point.

"Havoc always orders roasted chicken when we come here."

"Shut up, O'Sullivan," Havoc placed his hand over Serenity's. "I'm thinking about getting a pepperoni and cheese calzone." He whispered something to her friend that made her laugh.

"More wine," Lucky picked up the bottle and refilled their glasses.

Belle guzzled her drink. What was wrong with her? Nerves, it had to be nerves. Serenity mentioned sex, and well, Belle wondered if that might happen tonight with her and Lucky. Ripples of awareness shot to her core.

"We'll take another bottle," Havoc told the server who dropped off a basket of bread.

"Sure thing. You ready to order."

Lucky ordered for Belle seeing as they were sharing. He held the basket of bread for her. "Take one. It's really good."

"Okay." She slathered her bread with butter as he helped himself to two slices and passed the basket to Havoc.

When the main course came, she shivered in anticipation. Of what, she wasn't sure?

She twirled the fettuccini on her fork, and it fell off. She flicked her fingertips to use some of her dust to make the noodles stay in place. Darn Serenity for suggesting she mask her wrist emblem which disabled her magic.

Although she was right. Getting caught on Earth without permission would ruin both of their lives. A dark dungeon came to mind. Not that the council had done that to anyone, but they might. A cold chill went up her spine, and she shivered.

"You've gotta try the ravioli?" Lucky brought his fork to her mouth, and she took a bite.

Encased in pasta dough, the flavors of tomato and cheese erupted on her tongue.

"Told you it was good. How's the fettuccini?" His eyes were hooded, his voice oh so low and sensuous.

"Don't know." She fiddled with her noodles. "My fork's not cooperating,"

He grabbed it, did some sort of twirly thing with it, and made a tidy bundle.

"How'd you do that?"

"It's a top-secret trick." He handed it to her and helped himself from her plate.

Belle forked a ravioli, finished it, and speared a stalk of asparagus.

"Anyone want calzone?" Havoc asked.

"Why not?" Serenity seized a slice and picked off pepperoni. "The eggplant parmigiana is heavenly," she said with a sigh.

"Amore" played from the speakers. Plates were passed around, two wine bottles consumed. It seemed that Belle and Serenity's glasses were filled more times than the men.

"There's a bar down the street that has a live band." Havoc tilted his head toward Serenity.

"Absolutely," Serenity said. "You guys want to come?"

"Thought me and Belle might take back some dessert back to my place and watch a movie." He turned to her. "Would that be okay?"

"Only if I get to pick the movie." The movie didn't matter to her. Alone time did.

"Whatever you want?" He took her hand. His touch caused a spark to ignite inside her. Holy heavens, the mortal had pizzazz.

Ten o'clock on Saturday night. No shift at the bar. A pretty woman on the back of Lucky's bike. Life didn't get much better.

He pulled into the driveway when his phone beeped. "Geezer wouldn't call tonight unless it's important." He spotted Gran's icon. "Farryn's having her appendix out."

He read the text again. "This can't be happening." His throat closed, and he struggled to breathe.

"Where is she?" Belle spoke.

"The hospital." His sister was in the hospital. He texted his grandmother. "Tranquillity. It's just up the street."

"You should go to her."

"You're right. I have to get there." This was serious. More than serious. She was going under the knife. Panic gripped him. His heart thumped against his chest.

"If you don't mind, I'd like to go with you."

"Sure." He didn't turn to look at her and took off. His sister could die. No, he wouldn't let that happen to her.

When he parked near the emergency entrance of Tranquility Hospital, Belle got off the back, and they raced inside the double doors. A wave of fear shot straight to his heart. He couldn't lose his sister.

"Gran," he said, taking the seat next to her. "Is she okay?"

"Still in surgery."

"What happened?" Belle put her hand over his.

"Farryn came from the carnival holding her stomach and

crying from the pain. Felt her head. The poor dear was burning up, pale, lethargic. I wasn't taking any chances and loaded her into the car and brought her here." Gran looked wane, fragile. "The doctor told me the appendix hadn't burst. Said it was a good thing I didn't wait. She should be fine once the appendix is removed."

"That's a relief." Lucky let out the breath he'd held and slowly released it. "How long do you think it'll be before we can see her?" Deep in his gut, he felt guilty about his entertaining evening. He should have been there for his sister. He'd abandoned her again. He knew it was illogical but … bad things happen. Still, he couldn't help but think there had to be something he could have done to prevent this. And while he knew he didn't cause his sister's appendix to act up, he hated to be helplessly sitting there.

He should be with her, holding her hand. He should have been there and taken her to the hospital, not Gran.

"I know that look." Gran put her hand over Lucky's. "There wasn't anything you could've done to stop it."

How'd she know what he thought?

"Lucky's very protective of Farryn." Gran's said to Belle.

"Since our parents were too busy fighting, I had to step in." Except he hadn't kept his word to safeguard her when he split at eighteen.

"He must've been about eight or nine when he came with his sister for a weeklong visit. Farryn got stung by a bee in the backyard, and he carried her inside screaming for help."

"Gran has a habit of exaggerating things." He gave Belle a weak smile

"You love me anyway," Gran patted his hand.

"Not if you keep telling embarrassing stories about me."

"I like your stories, Gran. Shows Lucky's a good human."

He bust out laughing. "Human. What are you, an alien?"

"Just a Cupid."

"Interesting." Gran lifted a brow.

A man in a white coat walked up to them.

Lucky clenched his hands and said a silent prayer.

"Everything went well," the doctor stated. "She's in recovery. You should be able to see her in about an hour."

"Thanks, Doc." Lucky shook his hand. Still, until he saw his sister, he wouldn't be able to relax.

"There's no sense having you two sit around. Why don't you go home? I'll call if anything happens."

"We'll stay. You should get some rest." Gran looked tired.

"Nonsense. I've got plenty of games to play on my phone while I wait."

"Okay. I'll take Belle to her hotel and be right back." A bike ride might take away some of his angst.

"I really don't mind staying." Belle gave him a timid smile.

"Lucky said you're leaving tomorrow. I hope to see you before you go."

Belle hugged her. "Me too."

"I'll be right back. Come on, Belle." He held her hand as they headed out. "I'm sorry to ruin your night."

"You didn't."

He rode away from the hospital with Belle on the back. The motor's vibration didn't help to soothe him.

At the hotel's front entrance, he said, "I appreciate you being there with me."

"I didn't mind. I like your sister."

"Next time you're in town, I owe you dinner and a movie."

"If I'm back here again, I'll hold you to it, buddy." She put her hands on her hips.

"Has anyone ever told you you're adorable when you're snarky?" Without hesitation, he crushed his lips against hers for a brief moment and pulled away. "I'm curious what kind of movie you'd pick."

"Romantic comedy." She cocked her head, giving him a slight smile.

"Figures." No wonder she got along with Farryn and Gran so well. He couldn't resist one more kiss. He didn't want to let her go, but he had to be there when his sister woke, so he stepped back. "Call me when you're in town."

"If I'm back in town," she said.

"You'll come back, princess." He kissed her cheek and strode toward his bike. When he pivoted to see her one more time, she had disappeared inside.

CHAPTER 20

Monday evening in Cupid's Corner

BELLE LOUNGED on her couch drinking ambrosia. "What a great weekend."

"I had such fun." Serenity relaxed in the daisy chair. "Too bad you had to cut your Saturday night short with Lucky."

"Well, I did get to see him before I left." Restless the next morning, she had decided to visit his sister and found Lucky asleep by her side.

"I still can't believe I told Havoc to take me back to the hotel on Saturday night, rather than go to his place." Serenity had this faraway look. "What a dumb move."

"You did the right thing."

"Did I? Because I can't stop thinking about him. I might go back next weekend."

"Honestly? He's a mortal."

"But I really like him."

"If you chase him, he'll run." Belle learned that lesson in high school. She'd dated a cute Cupid on the track team, pandered to his every whim, including sleeping with him, only to be dumped in front of his friends. Cursed chaos, the memory still stung,

"You're right." Serenity set down her drink.

"Besides, a full moon aided our ascent, but next weekend there will only be a crescent showing."

Serenity let out a soft whimper. "Since you're taking your vacation soon, guess I'll have to live vicariously through you. I'm assuming you'll spend all three weeks on Earth."

"To try and find my aunt."

"Seeing Lucky will be an added bonus."

"Oh, yes." It'd been a little over a day, and she couldn't wait to spend time with him again. "Back to my relatives, did you have any luck hacking into Zinnia or Troy's file?" She crossed her fingers.

"None. It's weird. Someone or something is blocking access. I've dealt with locking codes and binding spells, but this one's above my abilities. It's as if a powerful magic encrypted into anything related to your aunt."

"Speaking of unreadable, I forgot to tell you about this." Belle rushed into her room and got the scroll from the bottom drawer of her dresser. "I found this underneath a false drawer in my parents' attic. Whatever it is must be important, otherwise, it wouldn't have been hidden. I can't read it. Can you?"

"Maybe." Serenity said. "Do you have any blank paper?"

Belle grabbed a couple of sheets of vellum from her desk.

Serenity swirled her coppery dust over the scroll and directed the dust to land on the paper and formed a copy of the scripted message.

"You're incredible."

"Keep your wings crossed that the next step works." Serenity tapped the paper with her fingertips. The characters changed into English.

"You did it.

They silently read it.

Every fourth generation, a pair of half-mortal cherubs shall be born into a dynasty whose name means a natural stream of water. One shall be ordinary. The other gifted with magical powers. Upon the noon hour on the twenty-fourth birthday, the gifted one shall become a multiplier, able to enhance the power to the beloved within one's sovereignty.

"WHAT A STRANGE PASSAGE," Belle said.

"Pair born on the same day must mean twins."

"I've never heard of any twins in my family. Still, given the secrecy behind Aunt Zinnia, anything's possible."

"It says there are twins every fourth generation. I wonder which generation you are."

"I have no idea. What if I'm the twin?"

"Why would you say that?"

"I had an imaginary friend who looked just like me."

"That doesn't mean anything. I did the same thing," Serenity said flatly.

"I guess it's just a coincidence." But the idea she might have a twin sounded awesome. "Last night, I couldn't sleep and decided to go through a keepsake box I'd stashed in my closet."

Serenity picked up her baby book from the coffee table and flipped through several pages. "Most of the book is blank. When I asked my mom, she blew me off by saying she'd been so busy with two toddlers to do much, but she managed to put plenty into my sister's pages." It irked Belle that her mother acted like her concerns weren't important, and when Belle asked for answers, Mom became annoyed.

"Look at those chubby cheeks. You were an adorable cherub."

"It's odd. The background has rubber duckies but not a single heart or bow and arrow?" Belle let out a long huff. "Plus, I'm smiling. Every other baby photo I've seen shows me either crying or fidgeting."

"You're not centered but off to the right."

"I hadn't noticed that." Belle gave her a plush animal. "I'm holding this unicorn. I know this sounds crazy, but whenever I hold this toy, it calms me." Until yesterday, Belle hadn't thought about this weird connection with her unicorn.

"Let me see it." Serenity ran her fingers along the fur, shook it, and held it up to the light. "Nothing seems unusual."

"Then why do I have a feeling there's something more to it?"

Serenity brought the stuffed animal close to her. She jiggled it. Turned it over. Examined the seams. Pulling on a string, the stitching came apart, and a key dropped to the floor.

"Where in Hades did this come from?"

"It probably belongs in the human world. Might open a safe deposit or post office box." Serenity's infinite knowledge continually amazed Belle.

"What's this number mean?" She called up Claire.

"Don't try searching here." Serenity grabbed Belle's wrist. "You might be tracked by the server."

"Close Claire," Belle said quickly.

"Hmm—" Serenity examined the label on the unicorn. "Handmade in Dreamland, California. It's a long shot, but you may find answers about the key there."

"I think it's close to Friendly Valley." She'd spotted a sign for the town on her ride with Lucky.

"You'll have to get Lucky to take you there."

Riding on the back of his bike would be the silver lining to her otherwise confusing turn of events.

~

LUCKY CAME into his grandmother's kitchen exhausted because Belle, a sleep-stealing beauty, invaded his dream. They were at the lake, and she wore a bikini and ran into the water with him close behind. She turned and splashed him, her eyes glittering with mischief. He closed their distance and pulled her into his arms ready to tease her lips with his mouth. Then he woke.

This was insane.

Their relationship consisted of two weekends in town, but she'd gotten into his psyche. He'd met plenty of women who appreciated Harleys, a few that rode bikes, but none that had Belle's mechanical aptitude and sassy sexiness. He hadn't seen her in a couple of weeks. Because his sister landed in the hospital, their date's end had been less than ideal.

Last night Belle called to say she's in town, and he'd invited her to breakfast. Knowing her sweet tooth, he'd made chocolate chip pancakes. During her last visit, they'd cooked together. As compelling as that had been, he'd rather take her out riding. Who was he kidding? He wanted to be alone with her.

"What's up with you?" Gran asked while beeps and whistles sounded from a game on her phone.

"Belle's coming over." He stacked two pancakes on a platter.

"That's marvelous."

While he agreed with Gran, her upbeat tone grated on his oh-so-wound-up nerves.

Ding-dong.

Startled, he flipped a pancake onto the floor and froze.

"I'll get the door," his sister called from the living room. "When did ya get in town?"

"About two a.m.," Belle said. "You look a lot better than last time I saw you."

"I was pretty out of it in the hospital."

"Glad you're all right."

"Me, too. I'll show you my scar later if you want." His sister wore that scar like a badge of honor.

"That's okay."

"Come on in, Lucky's making pancakes," Gran motioned her toward the table.

"I supposed I could sample one or two."

He turned as Belle removed her short denim jacket, hung it on the rack, and gave him a wide smile.

"You planning on feeding us?" Gran said, chuckling.

"Hush or I'll feed you that one." He picked up the dropped pancake, threw it in the trash, and brought a platter to the table.

Belle's mouth quirked up. "How's that Sportster coming along?"

"Almost done, just need to rebuild the clutch, and it'll be ready." Once he figured out the bugs, the bike would be perfect for a beginning rider.

"Any news on your aunt or uncle?" Gran asked.

Belle eased into the chair next to him. "I found this key

but am clueless what it unlocks." She reached into her jean's pocket and handed the key to his grandmother.

"It has a serial number. When we're done with breakfast, let's see what we can find on the internet." Gran passed the key to Lucky.

He got out his keys. "It's too short to be a post office box." Wondering where the key might lead, in his experience secrets led to misery. At nine, he'd been too young to understand his mother had an affair, but old enough to comprehend that she shouldn't be kissing a man who wasn't his father. A month later, she ran off with the guy. To this day, his gut still clenched. If he'd told his father, maybe his mother wouldn't have left.

"Where'd ya find the key?" His sister tilted her head.

"Sewn inside an old stuffed animal of mine." Belle drenched her pancakes in syrup and savored a bite. Did she notice his taunt expression, his tongue hanging out like a dog waiting for a bone?

"Reminds me of a Hallmark mystery movie," Gran said.

"Then my case will be solved in a few hours." Belle's hand brushed along his leg. Her mere touch made his body scream.

"One could only hope." Gran nodded.

He got up and refilled his coffee.

"What will you do if the key unlocks a briefcase full of money?" Farryn poured more syrup on her pancakes.

"You've been watching too many detective series, sis." She and Gran were recently hooked on crime mysteries.

"Don't be pessimistic. It could happen." His sister sipped her coffee.

"Back to the stuffed animal. Were there any other clues?" Gran picked up her plate and rinsed it in the sink.

"The toy was made in Dreamland." Belle gazed at Lucky and flashed a smile.

Oh hell. She had a beautiful smile—and a sensuous mouth. If he kissed her right now, she'd taste like chocolate and maple syrup.

"I remember seeing that town on our ride to Friendly City."

"The town's about two hours northeast of here." He set his arm on the back of her chair and skimmed his fingertips along the nape of her neck.

Gran picked up the key from the table. "DRB. Could be from Dreamland Bank? If everyone's done, why don't we head to the living room?"

"Okay." Belle glanced sideways at Lucky. Her pretty eyes glimmered. She settled on the couch, and he eased next to her.

Gran typed on her computer. "The bank's changed hands —now it's affiliated with Merger Bank." She pulled out her phone. "Do you want to call?"

"Could you?" Usually full of confidence, Belle sounded a bit squeaky. He reached for her hand and weaved their fingers together.

"I'll put us on speakerphone." Gran dialed and connected to a male clerk. "Hello, sir. I'm hoping you can help us. My friend recently found a safe deposit key from her mother's belongings and wanted to see if it matches any of your boxes. The number is seven-four-six."

"We have a box with that number. Please tell me your mother's name," the clerk said.

"Zinnia Brooks Andersen." Gran batted her eyelashes even though the clerk couldn't see her through the phone.

"It matches our information. If you care to come in, we're open 'till three today and from ten to five on weekdays." The clerk cleared his throat. "We'll need to see your ID."

"Of course. See you soon." Gran hung up, grinning like a Cheshire Cat. "Let's keep our fingers crossed that the key opens that box."

"It will. I just know it." Belle's face glowed with excitement. "It's quarter past ten. There's plenty of time to drive out there."

"If you want company, I wouldn't mind taking you." Lucky should be able to get someone to cover his shift tonight, and he had Sunday and Monday off.

"Only if we take your Harley."'

"You've got it." He found himself smiling.

"Before you leave, I did some searching in newspaper archives and found something interesting in the birth announcements." Gran sifted through a pile of papers on her desk. "Here it is." Gran's info might rock Belle's world and not in a good way.

"Bluebelle Bree Anderson." Belle stared at the announcement. "I have a cousin with the same first name as me.

"It appears that way," he said quietly, allowing Belle time to process what had been written in the paper.

"Born on June seventh, that's my birthday." Her face flushed. Uncertainty flickered in her eyes, her mouth thinned. "The name on my birth certificate is Bluebelle Breezy Brooks. It's really close to mine." She looked at him with confusion. "This can't m-mean … could Zinnia be my mother?

He nodded.

"This can't be." She seemed to be hyperventilating.

"Take a deep breath, princess," Lucky said, slow and steady. "Exhale."

"There was another child born. Blake Benjamin Andersen." She stopped, trying to process this info in her mind.

Another child was born on the same day as her. He shared the same parents. Her pulse beat so fast she felt dizzy. "Does this mean I have a twin sibling."

"It's possible."

Her face grew as pale as the printout in her hand. She slumped against him, and he had no clue what to do next.

CHAPTER 21

Belle came to with head against Lucky's shoulder. He raked his fingers through her hair, his brows creased. She stared at a copy of a birth announcement. Life as she knew it—filled with misinformation, deception, lies.

The memories flooded back. Could her mother be a banished Cupid on Earth? Her father—a human?

That would make her a hybrid-human. A half mortal with magic. Her twin brother might be ordinary. The legend from the scroll seemed to be talking about her.

No way! All this thinking hurt.

"Drink this." Farryn handed her a glass of water.

She scooted forward, and a dizzy sensation followed.

"Easy there, princess." Lucky steadied her from behind her shoulders. The simple touch tugged at her heart. According to Serenity, humans, and Cupids frequently had relationships. Zinnia had slept with Troy Andersen and had twins.

One of them had been her.

Nothing made sense.

Taking in several deep breaths, her lightheadedness had diminished.

"You better lie down in our guest room." Gran motioned toward the hall.

Sleep wouldn't change the newest information or the possible complications. "I'd rather learn what my key unlocks."

Belle glanced at the wall clock. "It's not quite eleven. If you don't mind, I'd like to leave soon."

"Sure, but I'd reconsider those shoes." He eyed her high heeled sandals.

"Since my sandals are new, I left a pair of sneakers in my car."

"You were hoping we'd go riding?" His eyebrow quirked.

"And if I was?" Flirting made things seem normal, at least for a second. "Actually, I checked out of my room just in case I found a lead."

"Get your stuff. I'll meet you out front."

Minutes later, she changed her shoes and held her fully stuffed backpack. He polished the mirror on his Harley. His leather jacket molded to his incredible biceps. "Hey." She moved beside him and rubbed her hand over the manifold covering the engine.

He snagged her into his arms. His warm mouth teased

her lips until he pulled away grinning. "Had to get that out of the way."

"You act like I'm a chore you had to get done." Belle pretended the kiss hadn't affected her, but to be honest, her pulse sped faster than a toy top. Lucky brought out a desire so deep it scared her. She wanted him more than any male she could remember.

"Works for me." The rascal grinned far too widely.

She still had the rental keys in her hand. "Think I could leave these here. I'd hate to misplace them, plus there's a chance I might not come back. In that case, I'm hoping one of you would return the car."

"Consider it done." He plucked the keys from her. "What about your luggage?"

She pointed to her stuffed backpack. "I managed to fit everything in here."

"A woman that packs light. Are you for real?" He smiled, causing those darn dimples to form.

"Just a figment of your imagination."

"Okay, smart ass. I'll be right back." He ran inside.

She stared at him. Her heart thumped.

It took him seconds to return. He picked up her bag, secured it with a strap onto the back of the bike, and hopped on.

She set her boots on pegs, wrapped her arms around his waist, and they rode off. She leaned into him. Familiar vibes made her happy inside.

She adored riding with him, taking in a swish of greasy

air. The engine roared while coasting along the highway. Passing fields and pastures and farmhouses, they continued north. The sun warmed her. The weather couldn't be more ideal. The day perfect.

Except, Aunt Zinnia might be her mother. She might have a twin brother. The people who raised her weren't her biological parents. Her whole life was a lie. Unbelievable.

"You cold," Lucky shouted.

"No." Uncertain, scared, curious, but not the least bit cold.

One thing about riding along the open road, she could ponder and analyze her life. Even as a little girl, she sensed something was off in Cupid's Corner. Everyone else in her family was blonde with blue eyes. She had red hair and violet eyes.

Taller than her friends, she longed to be little and petite. And in archery class in high school, even the worst archer could hit the white edge around the target. When she aimed and pulled back on the bowstring, she'd managed to bruise her forearm as her arrow embedded into the ground. She obviously hadn't inherited her mother's archery talent. In second grade, her teacher took pity on her and sent her to assist the kindergartners. That's how she met Cami. There seemed to be an immediate bond.

After years of taunting, innuendos, and feeling like a misfit with her classmates, being a hybrid would explain a lot.

A lump formed in her throat. If Zinnia was her mother, why had she given her up and kept her brother?

Don't go there. Wait to see what's inside the box.

The miles whirled by as they zoomed along the two-lane highway. The fresh air and constant speed invigorated her soul—while worry nagged her mind. She hugged Lucky a little tighter. His muscles flexed.

"Loosen up, princess, I still need to breathe."

She heard a chuckle in his tone

They reached the turnoff for Dreamland. "Another ten minutes or so and we'll be at the bank."

"Great." Her silly stomach knotted.

He stopped at a signal. The engine sputtered, spit, and stalled.

"Not again." He pulled to the side.

"What's wrong?" She had to get to the bank in time, and sucked in a deep breath, trying to remain calm.

"She's being temperamental. I need you to get off, while I try to get her to work. Usually takes a couple of kicks."

"Her?"

"Like a woman, she can be unpredictable. Makes life interesting." He kicked the starter. The engine coughed. Kicking two times, the motor engaged.

Belle let out a long sigh.

"Hop on." He popped the clutch, and they took off.

Passing a gas station, a couple of fast food restaurants, and strip malls, Lucky putted into a parking lot and parked in an empty space near the entrance.

She hopped off, clinging to Lucky's hand as if he were her personal life preserver. Would the key unlock any other shocking secrets? Well, she'd find out soon enough.

"You've got quite a grip there."

She let up on her hold.

"In your shoes, I'd be just as edgy." Funny how his words calmed her spirit, sort of.

She concentrated on the three-story brick building. It appeared solid with a few cracks and some missing mortar. The cracks reminded her of her life, but in her case, the cracks were expanding fissures.

Inside, people waited in line for tellers behind a six-foot counter. Lucky led her toward a modern desk under a customer service sign near the back. They took the padded chairs in front of a clerk. She clenched her hands to stop them from shaking.

"We called earlier about this key?" Lucky said as Belle pushed the key across the desk.

The clerk pulled out a card from a cabinet behind him. "I need to see identification."

She handed him her fake ID. Made by magic, it should be good. Still, her heartbeat thumped in her ears.

The clerk nodded, gave her back her ID, and signed and dated a card for the safe deposit card. He had her write her name next to his. Above it, Zinnia had signed on April second, a little over a month ago. Was she expecting her to come? Zinnia must've hidden the key in her stuffed unicorn. Talk about confusing.

Lucky and she followed the banker to a metal door where he punched in a code. "Relax."

How could she relax when she had no idea what to expect?

With rows and rows of metal boxes, hopefully, one of them would give her insight. "746 is in the middle row." The clerk inserted his key. "Put your key in the slot. We need to turn at the same time to open it."

The lock clicked. The clerk pulled out a long drawer. "Follow me to a private room." He brought them through a door on the other side of the vault. When you're done, push the button to buzz me, and I'll return."

He placed the drawer on top of a narrow table and shut the door. The place smelled like mothballs. Yuck!

"You're trembling." Lucky put his hand over hers.

"I'm fine." She sucked in a deep breath and pulled out the top document. State of California, Live Certificate of Birth. "Bluebelle Bree Anderson."

"I prefer princess."

"The name's growing on me." Her lips curved upward. His attempt to lessen the seriousness of the moment was sweet.

"Whoever set up this box went to a lot of trouble. Maybe that letter will explain why." He motioned to the bottom of the box.

A yellowed envelope showed Belle penned with an extra flourish on the front. Her hands shook. The light seemed overly bright.

"Allow me." Lucky undid the gummed seal and handed her a letter.

"Would you read it aloud?"

"If that's what you want, sure." He unfolded the page.

Dear Bluebelle,

If you are reading this letter, you have discovered the key I sewed inside your favorite stuffed animal.

Lucky paused.

"Go on."

What happened to you, my darling daughter, is complicated. Your father and I never willingly gave you up. On your first birthday, you were stolen from us.

"Someone kidnapped me. Oh my gosh!" She grabbed the letter and read it out loud.

You have been in our thoughts every day. Your father and twin brother, Blake, and I, long to see you again.

. . .

A TEAR DRIPPED down her cheek. People who she'd didn't recall cared about her. Not just people, her family. Beyond preposterous, unreal.

I've listed my phone number below and hope you will call me. There is so much to explain. Know that your father and I love you and always have. We never willingly gave you up.

Your loving mother

Please call 213-555-5555 or simply stop by 444 Red Rose Lane in Dreamland.

"UNBELIEVABLE. I was stolen from my real parents and twin brother." Her supposed parents loved her, they bonded with her. "I'm confused. Why would somebody do this to me?"

"I don't know. Hopefully, when you speak with Zinnia, you'll get answers. Any guess about who might have snatched you?"

"None."

"You have a twin. Didn't you sense a connection to him?"

"When I was little, I had an imaginary friend. A boy who looked just like me."

"Really? That's interesting." He held her hand. "Most twins have a type of telepathy. Did you?"

She thought for a moment. "Over the years, on occasion, I'd feel this sharp pain or sense danger with absolutely no reason. I didn't think much of it, until now." She jiggled the envelope, and a locket dropped into her hand. Inside, she found a baby picture of her on one side and her brother's portrait on the other. "That must be Blake."

"I'm not sure who was born first." Another stone cast against her life.

"Do you want to call Zinnia or just stop by the house?"

"I'd like to call but forgot my phone at my apartment." She didn't have one.

"You've got to be the only female in the world who isn't glued to their screen. Actually, I find it refreshing." He handed her his cell.

"It's oppressive in here. Mind if we go outside?" Air might help her process the information.

He buzzed the clerk to return. Moments later, they were outdoors. Lucky handed her his cell. Her adventure with him was finalized.

After she met with her real parents, the need for Lucky's help would be gone. A heaviness settled in her chest. Her world spun like a merry-go-round with no way off.

CHAPTER 22

Belle deserved privacy to make her call, so Lucky waited under a tall tree several yards away. Tension showed by her rigid stance as she held the phone against her ear. It couldn't be easy speaking with parents she had never known existed. They'd probably want to meet with her tonight.

This was a good thing. If things worked out with the Andersons, she might relocate here. He wouldn't mind the two-hour drive on occasion, preferring to keep things casual.

What would she want? Most likely commitment.

One thing he'd learned over the years, he sucked at relationships.

He stared at a heart-shaped cloud above. A sign, if he believed in such nonsense, which he didn't.

She came over to him. "No one answered. When I was

asked to leave a number on the voice machine, I froze and hung up."

"You have the address. Do you want to swing by?"

"If it's not too much trouble." Her skin turned pale as she gazed at him with worried eyes. "I'm numb."

"Of course you are. Learning about parents you never met it huge, but the idea of meeting them would make anyone apprehensive." He seriously doubted he'd handle such surprising news with her calmness. "You've had a lot thrown at you." He held her hand.

"And I dragged you into my crazy life." She looked at the ground as they walked. "Why am I so apprehensive?"

"It's only natural. Your mother's a stranger to you." Memories flooded back to him of his mom tucking him into bed and kissing his cheek. "I sometimes wonder what happened with my mom. She never returned. Farryn's been searching for her with no luck." He wished she wouldn't bother. Being left behind still hurt.

She gazed at him with empathy.

He couldn't stand being pitied.

Several minutes later, he pulled along the curb in front of a modest ranch-style house with pink shutters. "This is it."

They got off the bike. There were no cars in the driveway.

"How you holding up?" He placed his arm around her shoulders as they walked to the front of the house.

"I'm hanging in there." She rang the doorbell and waited on the porch. "Meeting my real parents is scary."

"The letter said your parents love you. Try not to worry." He attempted to be reassuring. The idea of being stolen and betrayed by the people who raised her sounded like something out of a movie. "Try knocking."

She did. Nothing happened.

The sun reflected off her wrist, and he ran his fingertips over a puffy silvery-purple shape. "Interesting tattoo?"

"Do you like it?"

"Never been much into hearts."

"You're funny."

He shrugged. "Try calling from out here. If anyone is home, they might pick up. Otherwise, you can leave a message."

She got out the envelope tucked in the front zipper of her backpack, and he handed her the phone.

"I can hear ringing from inside."

"So can I?" She pressed her lips together.

"It's obviously a landline. Don't forget to leave my number."

Once she left her message, they walked to his bike.

"It's frustrating to be so close." She rolled her eyes.

"Want me to take you to a hotel, or we could head back to Tranquility?"

"A hotel." Her eyes brightened. "You're brilliant. You'll stay with me, right?"

"If you want, we can get separate rooms." He thought it their best option.

"Or we could get one room with two beds. I'd rather not be alone tonight."

"If that's what you want." He wouldn't be sleeping with her, just giving her comfort. Life had thrown her mighty big punches. He could relate. Hell, his life punched him with plenty of uppercuts. The car that hit him broke more bones than he cared to count, but he survived. He shook off his wayward thoughts and used his phone to search for local establishments. "Sweet Dreams Hotel is just down the street."

"Perfect." Her voice came out soft, vulnerable.

"In the morning, we can swing by Zinnia's house on the way out of town and see if she's home."

"You're the best." She kissed him on the cheek, wearing a self-satisfied smile that lit up her eyes.

They rode a few miles south with her arms cinched around his body. He pulled into a parking space near the hotel entrance, got off, and escorted her through the lobby. It took maybe thirty steps to reach the check in counter and ask for a room with two queen beds.

Once inside the elevator, he pressed the third floor, the comparted jolted upward, and she fell into his arms. "This is cozy."

The brief contact shouldn't be simmering a fire in him.

The door binged open, and they followed the sign to the right.

"343. This is us." He placed the back of the key over the scanner, unlocked the door, and led her inside. "Why don't you take a shower? I'll call room service and order dinner."

"Sounds heavenly." She headed toward the bathroom.

He would've joined her in the shower if she asked. His stomach growled reminding him he hadn't eaten since breakfast. He looked at the menu on the nightstand. Pizza worked. He picked up the phone and ordered.

Moving to the window, he pulled open the drapes and gazed at a kidney-shaped pool below. A boy cannonballed into the deep end. A girl followed suit. A couple sat on chairs watching their children play. What was it like to grow up with normal parents? Parents who took their children on vacations and outings. Parents who put their kids needs first. He fought off the onset of melancholy.

Then the shower turned off, and he imagined a naked Belle. He snatched the TV remote from the dresser, pressed the power button, lounged on the closest bed, and channel surfed to a college baseball game.

A blow dryer hummed. The bathroom door squeaked. Belle came out in an oversized nightshirt that fell right below her knees. Lust burned all normal thoughts out of his brain.

She moved between the two queen beds, fluffed up the pillow next to him, and eased into the spot leaving a foot between them. "What are you watching?"

"Baseball." He couldn't resist stroking his thumb along her chin.

She snagged the remote out of his hand and stopped at a Star Trek movie. "You a Trekkie?"

"Never. How 'bout you?"

"Maybe."

"Admit it. You're their number one fan." He tickled her, and his hand ran across her breast. No bra. He swallowed hard.

"Something wrong?"

"Nope."

"Why don't you try to call from that phone? If you have to leave a message, you can tell her you're staying at the Dreamland Hotel, room 343."

"All right." She turned down the volume, picked up the phone, and called. "This ordeal's really messed with my head. I want answers now."

"I can only imagine."

A commercial came on for erectile dysfunction. "Change that, please?"

She left it on.

"You can be pretty obstinate." He rested on one elbow and brought his mouth against her velvety lips and sampled her lower lip with his tongue. "You taste like peppermint."

Someone knocked.

"Hope you're hungry." He got the door.

"Starved." She batted her eyelashes. What a flirt.

He sat, setting the box between them, handed her a can of root beer, popped his can of Coke, and reclined on the bed.

She picked up the smaller box on top. "What's in here?"

"Cinnamon bites."

"You're my hero." She picked up a ball and popped it into her mouth.

"That's supposed to be for dessert." He handed her a plate, set the box to the side, opened up the bigger box and grabbed two pieces of pizza. "Help yourself."

"My half's pepperoni." He bit into a piece. "This is good."

"And you got me veggie."

"Of course." He quickly polished off both slices and snatched more.

"This is kinda weird. I've never eaten in bed."

"And you think I have?" He drank the last of his soda.

"I didn't say that." She flashed him a smile.

"Right. Just so you know, I'll be sleeping on the bed without crumbs."

"Not hardly." She snatched the cinnamon treats and tossed the box on the other bed. "I'm more than willing to share."

"How mighty generous of you."

As she grabbed her purse from the floor between the beds, a paper slipped out of the front and landed on the comforter. "For a moment, I forgot all about this birth certificate."

He moved in next to her and took her hand. Chipped nail polish proved she wasn't prissy.

"I used to believe in following rules, but after this betrayal … well … thinking's overrated." Her fingertips ran up his arm to his shoulder. "Kiss me, please."

He trailed his knuckles along her cheek. Determined to take things slow, her floral scent distracted him. Her eyes filled with fire as he lowered his head, pressed his head against hers, and gently nipped her lip, coaxing her to open and swept his tongue with hers. He drew her closer, her breasts pushed against his chest, her body molded perfectly against his. Their tongues dueled in an inflaming game of desire. Sparks blazed through his veins and straight to his growing length. A soft groan escaped, and he was pretty sure it came from him. His hands slid across her back and dropped to her waist, feeling the heat radiating from her body. He pressed his hips against hers begging for her to ease this craving deep inside him.

He tore his lips from hers and trailed caresses along her throat. Her fingers twined through his hair. His hands roamed underneath her sleep shirt and cupped her bare bottom. Against his fingertips, her skin was smoother than satin. He wanted to explore each erogenous zone in her body. Her faint moans drove him with a need only she could fulfill.

Her hands slipped under his shirt, massaging his back, his skin felt scorched wherever she touched. He lifted his shirt off and tossed it on the floor. His breathing labored as he undid his belt buckle and unzipped his pants. "Tell me what you want?" His voice came out raspy.

"You."

His erection strained against his boxers as he lifted her nightshirt. In the wash of the lamplight from the nightstand, he gazed at her full breasts, her slim hips, her curves luscious and perfect. His hands ran over those curves, as he feathered kisses along her neck to one breast and scooted so his tongue twirled around the tip. He drew the bud between his teeth, blew on it, and the nipple hardened into a pebble.

Reveling with each little moan that escaped from her, his left hand slipped between her legs finding her wet. He dipped his finger inside, watching her violet eyes darken. His hard-on begged for release but pleasing her came first. His finger toyed with her, causing her to squirm. Using his other hand, he rubbed his thumb against her clit.

"Oh, Lucky." Her nails scraped along his back, as she bucked and shimmied. The fact that he made her come so quickly was a definite turn on.

He got off the bed, reaching for his wallet, anxious to bury his shaft inside her. "You want me to stop?"

"Heavens, no."

She was a goddess.

With a condom in his hand, he slid next to her in the bed. Her eyes focused on his cock making it twitch.

"I want you," he said, his voice hoarse. His hands shook as he unwrapped the condom and rolled it on. He rose above her. "You sure about this?

"Yes," she said in a breathy tone,

He entered her slowly, his eyes meeting hers as he filled her. Her warm core squeezed around him. Talk about nirvana. He waited, allowing her to adjust to his size. She wiggled her hips. He held her gaze as he started the rhythm that carried them higher and higher. Slow and steady. He drove faster, she matched him as he pumped harder.

He held back until she cried his name and rocketed with

an orgasm, following with his own shuddering release. His breathing still labored when he rolled over to the side. She splayed her hands across his back. For the moment, he'd found paradise in her arms, intoxicating and addictive.

He traced the tattoo in her wrist. It seemed to glitter brighter, but he figured it was a trick of the lighting. As he gazed at her flushed and creamy skin, he fiddled with a strand of her auburn hair fanned across the pillow. He should say something profound. What? He wasn't sure. For some sappy reason, he liked having her around.

And there lies the problem.

BELLE FELT Lucky's breath on her neck, a soft whistle in her ear, and a warm man spooned against her backside. Still in awe, she couldn't believe how many orgasms she'd experienced last night. Holy Aphrodite, the man knew how to make her body sing.

For someone who grew up in a community that promoted love, she turned out pretty clueless.

All she could gather was making love with him had been phenomenal. Not that she had much experience. Her senior year in high school, she'd slept with the track guy. He certainly hadn't turned out to be her soulmate or even a very good lover. She dated a few Cupids in college and slept with two of them. And with Wynton not once had she experienced anything remotely close to the euphoria Lucky had given her. If she were a hybrid that might explain the magnetism she had for Lucky. Her human side might be stronger than her Cupid side.

"Mornin'." Lucky shifted onto his side, his eyes darkening with desire.

Her body tingled with a hunger only he could release.

He growled as his mouth met hers. She admired him. He had to be the most exciting male existing on Earth. A simple sweep of his tongue had her lost in a spiral of yearning. Her hand drifted to his growing length.

His calloused thumb roamed to her breasts, making her moan as he played with her nipple. He peppered caresses along her neck. He inserted two fingers inside her core. Her lungs starved for oxygen. The slightest pressure would set her off. When he pinched a nipple, intense pleasure rippled through her.

"Your body is like a well-tuned motor."

Still coming down from that wondrous orgasm she thought she heard wrong. "Did you just compare me to an engine?"

"It's a compliment." His tongue flicked along her neck, her chin, her lips.

She skittered her fingertips down his back and cupped his butt. He rewarded her with a deep guttural moan. The kisses that followed claimed her, making her pulse skyrocket as their tongues danced and parlayed. Emotions soared and spiraled in a harmony of sensations. He touched and explored every curve and sensitive zone. His tongue darted in her ear, surprising and oh, so arousing.

When he pulled away, an emptiness filled her. A condom wrapper crinkled, and she licked her lips as he slipped it on. His huge cock was all hers.

"Like what you see?" A gleam accompanied his rakish grin.

"Yes."

"Good." He posed above her and entered her in one swift thrust. With him inside, the void that seemed to be a part of her everyday life disappeared, and she wrapped her legs around his waist to be even closer. He rocked her, moving slow, and withdrew, only to plunge deeper into her depths.

Flipping to his back, she straddled him similar to how she straddled his Harley—only better. She rode him for the long haul. His hands roamed along her breasts, his lips covered one tip, his teeth nipped.

"You bit me?" She said, her voice breathy and foreign.

He tried to reverse their position.

"Oh, no you don't." She liked being in control. She couldn't think, only feel. Each stroke became a little wilder and more frantic similar to pistons pumping faster and faster. Her core became hotter than the combustion of an engine, and she exploded. "I love you," her words slipped out on their own accord as he reached his own completion.

When the spasm stopped, she rolled off him desperate to escape. She couldn't believe she confessed her love. "I'm gonna take a shower." She thought maybe he'd want to join her.

"Go ahead." He wouldn't even look at her.

I didn't mean to say, "I love you." She told herself as she shut the door.

Tell that to her heart.

CHAPTER 23

Lucky walked through the lobby with Belle next to him and out the door. Why'd she have to spout the "L" word and complicate everything? Maybe she'd been on an emotional high for the moment. The sex had been incredible but had nothing to do with love and more to do with chemistry. Desire. Lust.

He liked being with her, but as far as love was concerned, he refused to go down that road again.

Preferring to put some distance between them, he'd promised to take Belle by Zinnia's house this morning. If her relatives weren't home, he'd be bringing Belle back to Tranquility. The thought made him anxious. His phone rang. "It's probably Zinnia."

"Yes, this is Belle," she said.

"No need. My friend and I were just about to head over

there." She gave him a wane smile. "See you soon." Handing him the cell, she said, "Let's go."

"Sure. You okay?" He got on, and she secured her position behind him.

"Why wouldn't I be?"

Because Lucky had barely spoken to her this morning. Plus, in a few minutes, she'd be meeting parents she never knew. He sucked in a deep breath as he rode along the main drag of Dreamland. He should be there for her, but all he could think about doing was dropping her off with strangers and running away. Giving her space. Plenty of space.

Within a few minutes, he pulled along the curb of the house with the pink shutters. "We're here."

"Already?" She said a bit terse and got off the bike. "You're coming with me, right?" Her apprehensive look reminded him of a deer caught unaware.

After shutting her out and acting like a jerk, how could he refuse? "Sure," he said when it'd be easier to slip away. Meeting her folks after a night of screwing their daughter—awkward. But she asked and knowing her situation, he couldn't refuse. He'd done as promised and brought her to her parents. If she and Zinnia clicked, he'd be on his way.

Those three dreaded words haunted him. Their relationship was supposed to be temporary. A fun fling with her living eight hours away in Heavenly Valley. Nothing serious. He should set her straight. Tell her he didn't do commitments anymore.

When? That wasn't the kind of thing to discuss with someone you'd spent only a couple of weekends with.

Hell. He was a first-class jackass.

Holding her hand had come naturally for him before. Now, the air swirled with turbulence. They reached the porch, the front door swung open. A petite blond woman rushed out and embraced Belle, holding her tight. "I never thought I'd see you again," Zinnia's words were choked as tears poured from her eyes. "My little girl has finally returned."

Lucky wondered if he could slip away and let the emotional scene play without him. He glanced at Belle, who stood stiffly in Zinnia's arms. Sneaking off right now would be a cowardly move.

"Your father will be beside himself he couldn't be here to greet you this morning. He's been in Chicago on business but should be home soon," Zinnia sniffled. "I still can't believe you're here." Zinnia eased her hold, and Belle moved away. "You're really here."

"Okay," Belle's voice rose an octave, something she did when nervous. Then her eyes darted his way. "This is my, um, friend, Lucky." A bit more than a friend after making love last night, should she have called him her lover? Absolutely not.

"Nice to meet you." Her mother used her fingers to wipe away the tears. "Both of you, please come inside."

"Of course," Belle said.

"I can only stay for a few minutes. Then I'd better head back." He followed Zinnia and Belle inside the house.

Belle turned and stared at him as if looking for reassurance, but he let his eyes stray toward the mantle. He gazed at a photo of a young man in a Marine uniform. The soldier resembled Belle.

"You have no idea how long I've waited for this day." Zinnia sniffed. "I never thought I'd ever see you again."

"I wish I had known about you."

"I'm sorry you didn't." Zinnia reached for a tissue from the box on a coffee table and pressed it against her dripping face. "We've got a lot of catching up to do. Most of it better wait 'till your father gets here."

In the living room, they passed a watercolor painting with a lake surrounded by a lush field full of colorful flowers. Belle stopped and admired it. "That looks like Lake Aphrodite."

He'd never heard of the place.

Zinnia squared her shoulders. "I painted it from memory."

They continued into the kitchen. Lucky pulled out a Windsor-style chair for Belle. White mugs were on fuchsia placemats. The floral centerpiece had a large box of tissues next to it.

"Would either of you like iced tea, coffee, or soda?" Zinnia asked, as she grabbed a tissue and dabbed her eyes.

"Coffee for me."

"Root beer if you have it."

"That's Troy's favorite drink." Zinnia's eyes misted as she poured him coffee and set a cup in front of him. She smiled at Belle with the same bow-shaped mouth, filled a glass with ice, and gave Belle a can of root beer.

"Would you like something to eat? I've set cold cuts, cheese, bread, and chips on the counter."

Lucky's stomach growled. Dammit. He'd never thought to have breakfast. "That would be great, Mrs. Anderson," he said.

"Help yourself." She turned and put her hand on top of Belle's. "I've lost so many years. You've grown into such a beautiful woman."

That was his cue to get some food.

"I'm struggling with this whole situation. I can't believe I have a brother."

He glanced over his shoulder. Belle wasn't crying, but he could see the confusion in her eyes. He'd never seen her so solemn.

"Where is he?"

"Blake's stationed in Colorado. He got his bachelor's degree in aerospace engineering and is training to be a pilot."

"Really. Did you encourage him to do this?"

"Possibly. He knows how I used to fly."

Zinnia had been a pilot. Why'd she quit? Whatever Zinnia did in the past was none of his business. With a plate in hand, Lucky eased into his chair. He ate his food. It could have been cardboard for all he knew.

"He knows about me? About everything."

"Of course. He can't wait to meet you." Zinnia's voice choked up.

"He wants to meet me?" Belle grabbed a tissue and dried her eyes.

"He does. We've all longed for this day. We'll be able to Skype with him later this afternoon."

"This is unreal. I have a brother, a twin." Tears streamed down her face.

Lucky felt like an intruder. It was time to leave. "Thanks for lunch." He drank the last of his coffee and stood. "I'd better get going."

"I don't know how I can ever thank you. You're an absolute angel for bringing my daughter home." Zinnia hugged him.

"I didn't do much." He pulled away. "Belle did most of the research. I just took her a few places."

"He's been great," Belle said with adoration in her eyes.

"Words can't describe how happy I am to have her back." Zinnia pulled out a tissue and blew her nose. "You have my family's gratitude."

Talk about being put on the spot. "I really better get going."

"I'll walk you out." Belle got up.

It hit him that Belle's problem had been solved.

She wouldn't need him anymore.

He should be relieved, not have this dumb ache knotting his gut.

Belle noted distance between her and Lucky. He didn't hold her hand as they walked to his motorcycle or drape his arm around her shoulders. At the curb, she expected him to kiss her as he had this morning, expected him to show he cared, expected reassurance. Instead, he leaned down, their lips met briefly.

"We okay?" she asked.

"You've got a lot on your plate. Get to know your family."

She wanted to ask if the *love* bomb upset him, but with her emotions in asteroid mode, the words wouldn't spill.

"I'm happy for you." His mouth brushed her cheek, and he hopped on his bike.

"What in Hades does that mean?" she said, but he'd started his Harley and drove off. It felt like a break up, except he was just a friend—a mortal lover and bed partner.

Belle used the walk to the house to quiet the bewilderment messing with her mind.

Zinnia stood at the front door waiting for her, watching her with a tender, maternal expression. For a moment, Belle faltered. The unconditional love that reflected in Zinnia's eyes stole Belle's breath.

They went into the living room.

Belle sat on the couch next to Zinnia and picked up a photo from the end table. "Is he my brother?"

"That's Blake."

"It's crazy to think I have a twin." She stared at the

brother she'd never known. Auburn hair and violet eyes. Belle stared at the picture again. For once, somebody looked like her. In Cupid's Corner, she had an older and a younger sister.

Wait!

Everything stilled and shifted.

They were her cousins.

It didn't make sense, nothing made sense.

Everything she knew about her family was a lie—her life was a lie.

How could she have a family on Earth?

Her mother pulled out a photo album. "Would you like to see your baby pictures?"

"Yes, please." Belle opened the first page to a young couple and squinted. The man wore a suit, the woman a lacey white dress. "Is that your wedding photo?" Zinnia must've been about Belle's age. The man with his arm around her must be Troy. He had the same eyes, the same hair coloring as Belle.

"It is. We were so young. With little money, we went to Big Bear and rented a cottage for the night. It was wonderful." Zinnia turned a few pages forward. "This was taken the day you and Blake were born."

In her arms, Zinnia held a baby swaddled in pink. Her father held the other wrapped in blue. Each parent brimmed with pride.

A sense of loss hit Belle. She had truly belonged with these people.

There were more pictures. Her mother had them dressed as pumpkins for Halloween. For Christmas, they wore red and white striped one-piece sleepers with matching caps.

"Does Blake know about my powers? That I'm a Cupid?"

"There are no secrets in this family."

"But plenty in the Brooks clan. Who kidnapped me?"

"My father. Your grandfather." The waterworks started again, and Zinnia grabbed another tissue.

"What? G-Dad? It can't be." Belle sucked in a deep breath. "He always seems to get me when others didn't." He'd been there for her when she came to the family estate crying because classmates made fun of her. He encouraged her to be herself and tinker with things, experiment, explore.

"Once I believed the heavens revolved around him. He fooled me by pretending he loved me."

"What do you mean?"

"Shortly after I turned twenty-two, I graduated from the Archer's Academy and started getting assignments on Earth. Everything went well until I had this difficult mortal who had major trust issues. I couldn't get her and her soulmate together in order to shoot a love potion arrow. So I asked my father for advice."

"And he persuaded you to take the mortal's man for yourself?" Belle knew full-well how G-Dad had swayed her to his side.

"What?" Zinnia cut her a surprised look. "He told me to befriend the woman." Zinnia folded her arms. "It wasn't uncommon for Cupids to transform for a couple of days.

Being a newbie, I was rather apprehensive. My father suggested I try, so I figured it'd be fine. And had a blast. I took line dancing at the Y with the mortal. We hit it off. By the end of the week, I not only had a friend but somehow managed to get her to give her boyfriend another chance. I transformed into my Cupid form and shot them with a love boost arrow. My mission was complete."

"Okay, this is going in a different direction than I thought. How'd you meet Troy?"

"I was hooked on the human experience. It was different from Cupid's Corner. There was no pressure. No Cupid's council judging. No townsfolk watching my every move. "

"I get that. Cupid's Corner can be rather stifling." Belle had been ridiculed for being different.

"I decided to spend a few more hours at the bar where we'd gone dancing with my new group of friends—all mortals. And Troy walked in. I was smitten from the second I met him, although thinking back, Father may have shot Troy with an arrow, but I was naïve. I mean, why would my father push me to be with a mortal?"

"It is hard to fathom."

"Maybe he didn't. But I find that highly doubtful." She sighed. "Anyway, I kept up on my assignments, but if they were close to Friendly City, I'd head there for a few hours at a time."

"What did Troy think about you coming and going?"

"I told him I did a lot of traveling for my job." Zinnia

sighed. "It didn't take long before I was hopelessly in love with him. Three months later, I found out I was pregnant."

"Don't tell me you told your mother?" Belle couldn't imagine telling Grand Dame that she carried a mortal's child.

"No way. She had loftier goals for me. Earlier that year, I had dated Henry Aphrodite a couple of times. When she noticed me getting sick in the morning, she had been giddy, certain that I'd marry into the Aphrodite family."

"I can only imagine." Grand Dame's station would have been elevated. "I dated Wynton Aphrodite. While she was polite to him, she didn't see any gain. After all, if we got married and had children, our offspring would be tainted with mortal blood."

"Did she take the choices I made out on you?" Zinnia gave her a half-smile.

"I survived." At least Grand Dame didn't like her for a reason. A lame reason, one that didn't make her animosity acceptable. As a little girl, her grandmother's disdain had crushed Belle, but as she got older, she learned to ignore the jabs and jibes.

"I suspect seeing you reminded her of my shortcomings. I was her big chance to improve our family's status." Zinnia stood and walked toward the fireplace.

"That's cold-hearted!"

"She wasn't always that way. Growing up, she often brought us to the shore to collect shells and swim or the edge of the forest to picnic." Zinnia squinted. "She brought me into this world. For that I am thankful."

"What happened when Grand Dame learned the truth?"

"She banished me from her house. I snuck back to Earth and told Troy about the pregnancy. He insisted on marrying me." Her mother had a faraway look. "He's a good man."

"Did anyone from the Cupid council come after you?" She wasn't sure how the process worked.

"My dad found me somehow. He said if I truly believed that Troy was my soulmate, he'd support me. He wanted me happy." She shook her head. "I should have been wary. My father always followed the Cupid rules, or so I thought. As an archer, he had the freedom to visit often during my pregnancy. Once you and your brother were born, he was ecstatic."

Belle stared at a photo of her and her brother. "We're both holding stuffed unicorns."

"We bought those for you when you were about three months. Neither of you could sleep without your Unis."

"That's weird because I called my stuffed animal Uni." Belle flipped through the pages with longing for a life she didn't have. Her heart slammed with anger. "I recognize this photo, except mine didn't show my brother."

"You and Blake were about ten months old them. That's when my father made weekly visits." Tears filled her sapphire colored eyes. "I thought he enjoyed playing with you two. In reality, he was watching both of you for signs of magic."

On a cherub's first birthday, the presence of a heart

emblem announced magical abilities. The wings developed shortly after that.

"Troy warned me. Thought your grandfather had an ulterior motive. Turns out he did." Her mother choked up. "The week before your birthday, he said if either of you were gifted with magic, it'd be best to raise you in Cupid's Corner, I informed him both my cherubs would be raised right here."

"Good for you." Belle liked that her mother stood up for herself. She stood up for Belle.

"My father tried to patronize me by saying, 'Don't worry, the chances of having a hybrid child with magic are slim.'"

This seemed surreal. The kindly man she loved was an imposter.

"Troy and I decided to stay at a hotel for the next week and not let either of you out of our sight." She grabbed a tissue and wiped the tears from her cheek. "We didn't know if either of you would have magic, but we still worried about my father's threat. Troy came up with the idea of sewing a key inside each of the stuffed animals, just in case."

"That's how the key got there." Belle fought over her anger. "I never would have found you if you hadn't hidden the key."

"But here you are, my sweet little Bluebelle." Zinnia blinked several times. "I have to quit blubbering, but I can't seem to help myself. I'm just so happy."

Belle wished she felt the same, but she struggled with her anger at G-Dad for snatching her away from the life she had deserved. "What was I like as a baby."

Zinnia's gaze softened. "You and your brother were happy—both of you full of wonderment and awe."

"I've never thought of myself as happy." She stared again at the photo of her and her twin grinning with only a few teeth as they held unicorns.

"You were. And sweet and loving and the very best." She dabbed her eyes. "You had this special babble that only the two of you seemed to understand."

"That's incredible." She wished she could remember.

"The night before your first birthday, a faint heart tattoo formed on your wrist, and not your brother's. Proof you inherited Cupid magic. Your dad and I knew it would be a challenge keeping your gift from others, but we were determined to give you a normal life."

Dad? In her mind, her Uncle Cole still represented her father. How messed up was that?

"I have to show you something." Belle reached in her backpack for the message she'd found. "It'd been encrypted inside a scroll. My friend, Serenity, transferred the calligraphy to paper and changed the characters into English."

"She sounds like a phenomenal friend."

"She's brilliant and full of fun." It would be nice to have Serenity here right now.

HER MOTHER READ the message out loud.

Every fourth generation, a pair of half-mortal cherubs shall be born into a dynasty whose name means a natural stream of water. One shall be ordinary. The other gifted with magical powers. Upon the noon hour on the twenty-fourth birthday, the gifted one shall become a multiplier, able to enhance the power to the beloved within one's sovereignty.

"WHERE DID YOU FIND THIS?"

"Underneath a secret compartment inside a desk drawer in my parents' attic. Now I get the line, *'One shall be ordinary, the other gifted with magical powers.'* That refers to Blake and me. G-Dad didn't kidnap me so I could have a better life, he wanted me to multiply his own powers." Her chest tightened, her pulse raced. Not only did rage flow through her veins, but a strong sense of resentment at the unfairness of it all made her head ache.

"I'm sorry, Bluebelle."

"Me, too. He hurt us all."

"He did."

"If you were in the hotel with Blake and me, how did he kidnap me?"

"The morning of your birthday, I woke to find you in your grandfather's arms." Her lips quavered. "He said my older brother agreed to raise you. I told my father you weren't going anywhere. Father insisted it'd be risky to have you remain on Earth. Insisted you needed training to learn to control your magical abilities in Cupid's Corner. I still said, 'NO!'"

"He said you'd have a happy life. I pleaded to let you stay. He promised I could visit you anytime, but moments later, he transformed himself and you into Cupid sizes and flew off with you. I tried to stop him, but my magic had dissipated within a week after I decided to stay in human form. I think it has something to do with the Earth's magnetic pull in relationship with the larger stature."

Belle glanced down at her wrist. "Why do I still have my ability?"

"I don't know. Maybe because you're half mortal."

The truth slammed in her mind. Belle belonged to two worlds—she belonged in neither world.

"Without magic, Troy and I had no way to go after you."

"Didn't you create extra magical vials before you left Cupid's Corner?"

"I wish I had."

"I have vials in my backpack." Belle had been prepared.

"I'll keep that in mind."

"What happened after I was stolen?"

"My father crushed our world. We couldn't contact the police or tell anyone that my Cupid father flew off with my daughter."

"What'd you do?"

"Survived. Barely." Zinnia placed her hand on top of Belle's. "We had to go on because of Blake. He constantly cried for you. He didn't understand why you were gone."

"My mother, I mean … Aunt Opal and Uncle Cole perpetuated the lie. How could they live with themselves?" She wanted to despise them for what they'd done.

"Cole had always been a good brother. We were close. When I decided to marry Troy, he refused to visit me." Zinnia folded her arms. "But don't blame him for what happened. Knowing my father, he told Cole that I wanted him to raise you. It must've been tough on Cole and Opal since they had a toddler of their own."

"Orchid. My oldest sister. Not sister, cousin." The lines of duplicity blurred all logic.

"I'm sorry."

"It's not your fault. And everyone in the family was fairly nice, except—your mother." Belle didn't exactly hate her, but she had a strong dislike for the woman. "Grand Dame must not have known about the scroll. If she thought I could multiply her powers, she might have been nicer."

"Given how the scroll was hidden, I doubt she knew anything." Again, Zinnia picked up the paper. "Or she'd be interested in improving the Brooks' bloodline."

If Cupids were the epitome of love, how'd her family end up so damaged? "Back to the message, I don't get this part, 'Beloved in one's sovereignty.' Sovereignty can signify rightful status, domination, supreme and independent power, or authority." Belle didn't care about dominating others.

"What if it means you'll have the authority to enhance the power of those who truly love you?"

"I hope you're right." The whole ordeal weighed on Belle.

"Don't fret." Zinnia squeezed Belle's hand. "If the message applies, you'll find out the truth on your birthday in two weeks."

"I've been busy all morning and just checked my cell's messages." A lanky man with hair the same deep auburn color as Belle's rushed inside. "Bluebelle, you're home."

She stood, and he held her in his arms. A warm, gushy feeling filled her heart.

"I can't believe you're actually here." His voice was choppy.

"Me, neither. Everything seems surreal."

"You have no idea how much I've missed you. We've all missed you." He stepped back with tears in his eyes. "It's been almost twenty-three years since I last saw you. Let me look at you." The love emanating from his gaze made her eyes get misty. "You're all grown up. Isn't she beautiful, Zin?"

"She's perfect, just like she was as a baby." Her mother sighed. "I've been showing her pictures."

Belle sat on the couch.

Her father moved to the empty spot on her left. "Have you talked with Blake yet? He's gonna be so excited."

"She just got here, Troy."

"Oh, right. Well, how'd you find us?" He pressed his lips together. "Knowing your grandfather, I doubt it was easy sneaking away."

"Actually, my best friend gave me pointers. Finding information was the hard part, but I managed."

"I'm glad you did." Her father wore a beaming grin.

"We're all glad you did," her mother added.

The lacking part in her became crystal clear. They wanted her. She could feel it down deep to her soul.

"I want to know everything about you. Learn about your hobbies. Your favorite things." He held her hands in his. "This must be overwhelming."

"It is." Her energy was draining fast.

"She thought Cole and Opal were her real parents."

"I'm not surprised, although I don't blame her brother. Her father had no right to kidnap you. He's an S.O.B."

"I'm learning that. Zinnia was explaining the details of my abduction right before you arrived." G-Dad had robbed her of the life she deserved. "How'd you cope?"

"We put on a brave face for your brother, but memories of you were everywhere. We stayed in Dreamland hoping for your return. Have you had a happy life?" Troy asked.

"I was loved." Lack of sleep mixed with a bucketful of emotions had her drained. "Could you take me back to the hotel?" She had enough money to cover a few more nights.

"If that's what you'd prefer, but we'd like you to stay in our guest room," Zinnia said.

She could see their hopeful expressions. They wanted her here. They wanted her. "All right." She still had plenty of questions, but right now she needed to be alone to process everything she'd learned.

Zinnia showed her to the back of the house and inside a decent sized room. A white comforter with red arrows covered the double-bed. "Make yourself at home." She cupped her face, and stared at her, before giving Belle a hug. "If you need anything, give me a holler." She left, pulling the door shut behind her.

Belle flopped onto the bed. Abducted at such a young age, she didn't have memories of her parents or her twin. She spotted another watercolor painting on the wall above the bed. Lake Aphrodite. Painting must've kept her mother's memories of Cupid's Corner.

Near the water's edge, a red-haired cherub holding a stuffed unicorn flitted. The little girl was Belle.

She found herself sobbing, crying for a life she should have lived, people she should have known, a world where she would have belonged.

CHAPTER 24

Three weeks later, June 12th

"I DON'T NEED ANYTHING ELSE," Belle said to Zinnia, after their shopping spree, they had facials and mani-pedis at a spa, and now headed to the hair salon.

"Are you kidding? You deserve to get pampered," Zinnia said. "Tomorrow, I'll get to spend the first birthday with you after twenty-three years." Love shone in her eyes.

After four weeks on Earth, Belle understood what unconditional love meant. It didn't matter to her parents if she fit in with society or how she acted. They loved her because she was their daughter.

Last week, she and Troy were restoring a seventy-six Camaro. Somehow, she'd managed to get grease on her hands, mechanic's overalls, and even smear it on her cheek. When she went inside the house to clean up, Zinnia didn't criticize or show disappointment. She burst out laughing. "Look at you two."

Troy was also a mess. Grease had splattered across his white T-shirt and even got into his hair. "What can I say?" He had chuckled. "She takes after me."

Belle discovered the missing link in her life here on Earth. Still, a part of her felt guilty being here when she'd always been a part of her Cupid family.

"Have you heard from that nice fellow, Lucky, who brought you here?"

"No. I thought I would by now." It hurt that he hadn't called.

"Does he know you're a Cupid?"

"No." The thought had crossed her mind, but she'd been too afraid to say anything. "What did Troy do when you told him?"

"He thought I was joking. When I showed him my Cupid form, he fainted." Her mother laughed.

"Wow." She couldn't imagine Lucky doing that. "But he accepted you?"

"We were in love, and he didn't want to lose me."

"Weren't you worried the council might find you and bring you back?"

"Definitely, but Troy is worth the risk. I would never be happy in Cupid's Corner without him." Her mom stopped at a light. "Your man will come around. Give him time."

No, he wouldn't. Lucky didn't love her. Belle pushed away the melancholy filling her heart. They were over. It was time to quit dwelling on him.

Her cell rang, and she dragged her phone out of her purse. She had finally got ahold of the right phone number for her friend, only to find out she was on her honeymoon and left a message. Finally, she'd talk to her BFF since grade school. "Hey, Cami. How's that cowboy you married?"

"Absolutely wonderful."

"Sorry I missed your wedding."

"Serenity was there. She said you were searching for a banished aunt. Did you find her?'

"She turned out to be my mother." Belle still found the ordeal unbelievable and upsetting. "It's a long story, and I only have a few minutes right now to talk. I'll call you later."

"You'd better. It's so good to hear your voice. Any plans for your birthday tomorrow?"

"Nothing much."

"I'd have Dusty drive me to see you, but things at the ranch are pretty busy right now. It'll be the first birthday I've missed since we met," Cami said.

"It's fine, really. Like you, I'm planning on staying on Earth. We'll get together some other time."

"I'd love that."

"Have you heard from Serenity lately? I was supposed to return home a week ago. Knowing her, she's covered for me, probably meddled with the department's computer system."

"With Zander's uncle on the council, I'm sure that Cupid

already knows about what I've done. If the council learn that you've snuck off to Earth, they might start watching Serenity closely."

Belle gasped. "I sure hope not."

"We're here," Zinnia said, as she pulled into the parking lot of Curls and Swirls.

"I'm getting my hair done, so I have to go. Call me later, like around seven, and we can catch up." Belle said, and Cami agreed.

"How's your friend adjusting to life on Earth?" Zinnia asked.

Over the last few weeks, Belle had shared things with Zinnia about her friends. "She sounds happy."

Belle walked into the shop. "Maybe I should get purple highlights in my hair."

Zinnia laughed. "You'll definitely stand out."

TODAY WAS BELLE'S BIRTHDAY. She woke and stretched her arms above her head. Sunlight filtered in through the lace curtains. The silvery sparkles in her wrist emblem were brighter than usual.

Pretty.

6:12 according to her clock—thirty-nine minutes until the exact time of her birth. An odd power surged through her, and she flicked dust from her fingertips. Her white comforter changed to hunter green with flashing white lights. Something strange was happening.

She searched through her closet for the new outfit she bought while shopping with her mother yesterday. She dressed in a royal blue halter top with matching shorts.

This should be a glorious day. She'd found her biological parents and had been staying with them. As supportive as her mother and father were, her heart ached for the lie she had been forced to live. She should have gone home a week ago. The lie she weaved had her worried.

Her mother would notice that Belle hadn't come back yet. Not mother—Aunt Opal. Knowing her, she would assume Belle chose to stay in Lover's Landing with Wynton, and that would make her aunt ecstatic. Had Opal hoped for a marriage to improve her family's station, one that would place the Brooks above the Eros family?

Her stomach clenched. A bigger problem was G-Dad. She was quite certain he'd want to use her inherited power to multiply his own and make himself stronger. As she thought back to her times spent with him, she realized his power was already at least three times her own. What if he forced her to return? She shivered.

Even though she'd miss the family she grew up with, especially her sisters, the lifestyle in Cupid's Corner held no appeal.

She knew in her heart she belonged on Earth.

G-Dad wouldn't care.

She shrugged. It was her twenty-fourth birthday, and she planned to enjoy ever minute.

With an electronic tablet she'd borrowed from her father in hand, she opened the sliding glass door in her bedroom and strolled out to a bench under a tall oak tree. She stared above at the dark, gloomy clouds, refusing to allow a few clouds to ruin her special day. It was her birthday. She wanted to celebrate with the only constant that stayed in her mixed-up life. She wanted the freedom of flying. What would it hurt?

Nothing.

Using her fingertips, sparkles twirled around her and transformed her into her sixteen-inch Cupid-size wearing a strapless satin dress. Her wings unfu rled from her shoulders, and she held the tablet against her stomach.

Flying above the yard, the house became smaller, the backyard greener. She soared in wide circles until she grew weary and perched on a branch near the top of a tree to ponder about her life.

Securing her tablet on her lap, she clicked on the *History of Harley Davidson Motorcycles* and swiped to a photo of a Knucklehead. Her thoughts again strayed to Lucky. She yearned to work next to him in his garage, yearned for their playful banter, yearned to wrap her arms around him as she rode on the back of his Harley.

Countless times she thought about calling him from her parent's phone but didn't. At first, she'd been too hurt to try. After a week, it was awkward. It'd been bad enough to beg him to stay in the room with her. Making love changed their casual dynamics. Saying, "I love you," had obviously ruined his mood. The next day when she asked if they were good, he didn't so much as blink, just left her to get to know her parents.

She was better off without him.

Lightning hit a few miles away. Her clue to head back home.

Unfurling her wings, she fluttered across the sky

A raven cawed in the distance.

Cursed cyclops! It's after me.

She flapped hard and fast, floated near the front of the house, and dropped to the ground. Wow! That was close.

She swirled her silvery violet dust. Her body grew, and she transformed into a fully dressed human wearing the halter top and shorts from earlier.

She came in the back doorway to the kitchen.

"Happy birthday." Her mother's face beamed as she embraced Belle.

"Thanks." Since her Cupid's Corner family hardly ever hugged, much less showed affection, these displays took some getting used to.

"You deserve the very best birthday." Her mother set a plate of blueberry pancakes topped with whipped cream on the table.

Belle had made blueberry pancakes with Lucky.

That cut right to her core. Lucky hadn't even bothered to call. Belle had tried to forget him, but lately, he'd been invading her dreams. She'd see the enamored look in his eyes, feel his lips pressed against hers, and after they'd make love, she'd thrown out the "love" bomb.

It's time to get over him.

"Hey, birthday girl." Her father walked in and kissed her cheek. "Yum, blueberry pancakes." He plunked in the seat next to her.

If she'd been raised in Dreamland, she and her twin brother would have this tradition to share. Panic shivered through her whole body. She always joined her mother ... no, her Aunt Opal ... for boysenberry crepes on her birthday. Even if they assumed she was with Wynton, she would question why she hadn't answered any messages on her heart emblem, unaware that she was on Earth with her real mom.

"The only thing that would make today better would be to have your brother here." Her mother said. Pink dust swirled from her fingertips, and a Skype call sounded on the open laptop on the counter. "Did I do that?"

"It wasn't me." Belle shrugged.

"My magic hasn't worked in years."

"Hello." Her dad clicked the accept button. "We were just talking about you, Blake. Happy birthday! How's your day going?"

"Thank you. Where's sis?"

"Right here." Belle stepped closer to the computer. She'd skype with her brother several times in the past few weeks, but it still amazed her how similar they looked. "Happy birthday! How's your day going?"

"Quiet so far. I'll be skydiving at noon."

"Next year I'm joining you." It would be like free-falling without wings.

"You're on." He fist bumped the screen.

"Be safe," her dad chimed in.

"I always am." He had the same laugh as Troy. Belle still struggled to think of him as her dad.

"Enjoy your birthday, I plan to do the same." Belle stepped away from the counter and began to eat her breakfast.

Zinnia and Troy kept on talking. They had a comradery, a closeness that made Belle long for the years lost. Zinnia, Troy, and Blake had a bond. They'd welcomed her whole-hearted into their family, but … it was so new. She was still finding her way.

The doorbell rang. Since her mom and dad were talking to Blake, she pushed away from the table to see who it was. Belle got the door. "Candy gram for Belle. He handed her a box."

The sender turned out to be Cami. She and her Cupid friends always sent candy grams. Serenity would receive hazelnut truffles. Cami-coconut divinity puffs. Belle's mouth watered as she opened the box. "Yes. Raspberry-caramel bonbons!"

She headed back into the kitchen. Her brother's face no longer showed on the computer screen.

"Yum." Her father reached for a candy

"You can have one, and only one." She slapped his hand.

"Is that from Lucky?" her mother asked.

She wished. Belle felt a twinge of melancholy. "Cami."

"If you'll excuse me for a moment, I'm going to call her."

"Absolutely, birthday girl." Troy snagged another candy from her box.

"You and your sweet tooth," Zinnia laughed.

Belle went into her room. No purse. When did she last have it? Yesterday shopping. "Think I left my purse in your car," she said to Zinnia.

"The keys are on the rack by the front door."

She grabbed the unicorn keychain. "Got it!" Standing on the front porch, the air felt heavy. Wind whipped her hair as she hurried down the driveway. Oppressive darkness filled the sky. Thunder boomed.

Her pulse ticked and ticked, as she unlocked the door to the Volkswagen bug, pulled the handle up, and grabbed the strap of her purse.

Lightning stabbed downward as she shut the door. The bolt hit the ground less than a foot in front of her.

A Cupid with glittery wings and a red suit materialized as an older human in front of her.

"G-Dad?"

"Happy birthday, Belle."

"Why are you here?" Anger seethed through her.

"I wanted to wish you a happy birthday and give you this." He held out a tiny red box and pressed the three-inch gift in her hand. In contrast to his grin, his sky-blue eyes glinted.

"As if I'd trust any item coming from you." She flung the

present on the ground. "I know you kidnapped me as a cherub."

"You've got that wrong." His right eye ticked. "Your mother wanted me to take you."

"Liar." She had no patience for his nonsense and pushed past him.

"You didn't belong on Earth." He reached for her, but she put her hands behind her back. "Zinnia understood this."

"As if she wanted to separate me from my brother. Go away."

"There's something you need to know about turning twenty-four."

"It'll be noon in less than an hour. That's when my powers will be in full force." She gave him a daggered glare, although shaking on the inside because she had no idea what to expect.

"How did you learn that?" He glowered.

"I found the scroll hidden in my supposed parents' attic." She stepped around him, not about to play into his games.

"You never should have snooped, never should have visited Earth, never should have learned about your mother."

"You're the one who removed her images from all the photographs?" Now things were beginning to make sense.

"I didn't want you asking questions."

"That's why I got the *beware* message when I opened my father's file."

"It was only meant to scare you."

It hadn't stopped her from wanting to know the truth.

"You stole me as a toddler in order to make *your* magic stronger. As if you need any more power. Your powers are already strong enough."

"It's not for me, Belle, it's for our Brooks family. With you, my special girl, we will have the ability to take the Eros clan down a peg."

"Our family will once again regain our position." He puffed out his chest, reminding her of a proud peacock.

He used to call her his special girl. She once trusted him more than anyone, but no longer. Her life would have been different, most likely happier if she'd remained on Earth. "As if I'd believe you. How can more magical power do that?"

"It's fairly straightforward, my dear, the Brooks archers will become the best in the land."

"You're already an elite archer. What do you personally gain from being around me?" She had to know.

"Charisma. With a bit more magic, the townsfolk will choose me as the council leader, thus dethroning the era of the Eros clan."

"I've been a pawn in a game of envy. You didn't care that I never truly belonged in Cupid's Corner."

"You are wrong. I have loved you from the moment I met you. I did what was best. You've always had a special hold on my heart."

She wanted to wipe that smug smirk off his face.

"There's something missing with this picture. I'm betting the rumors about my great great grandfather, Rufus, were true. He had an affair with a mortal. The rumors that ruined our family name were legitimate."

"It doesn't matter."

"Yes, it does." And he'd better tell her everything.

"If you must know, he had mortal twins whom he never acknowledged."

Rufus started a feud based on lies. She thought for a couple of seconds. "Those twins would have been born four generations ago."

"Yes. According to Rufus, his powers diminished not long after his twins would have been twenty-four, and then he lost his position on the council. If Rufus had seen the scroll, he would have brought the gifted twin to live with him, and our elevated status would have remained in tack."

"Like you did?"

"Exactly."

Belle wanted to punch that smug smile off G-Dad's face. How could he have been proud of kidnapping her?

"Four generations before Rufus, had a different set of half-mortal twins been born? Did the gifted twin enhanced the Brooks' power and elevate our status?" She had to know.

"It appears that way, but I'm not certain. I have yet to see any twins written in our family tree. Of course, any mortal offspring wouldn't be recorded."

"Of course." Cupids didn't sleep with mortals. It was forbidden. What a bunch of bull. "Why didn't Rufus see the scroll?"

"Someone had hidden the scroll in that roll top desk. If only Rufus had discovered it in time."

The desk that ended up in the attic where the Brooks family had lived for generations.

"Rufus hung onto the scroll, showing it to me when I was in his twenties."

"So you could make certain the family retained its former glory." Belle was totally disgusted with the whole thing.

"With you as the legacy." G-Dad put his hands on his hips and flashed a satisfied grin. "Cole and Pete were never interested in mortal relationships, but I figured Zinnia could be swayed. And now that you know everything, you, my special girl, will fulfill the prophecy."

"Not gonna happen."

He cleared his throat. "You're coming with me."

"Never." She stepped toward the house.

He grasped her wrist.

"I refuse to live in a world where my only purpose is to enhance the Brooke's name. I want no part of that life." She tried to twist out of his hold. "I'll never return to Cupid's Corner."

"You're coming with me." He swirled his magical dust.

"No, I'm not." She tried to push him away and couldn't move.

Her parents rushed out the door. "Belle," her mother yelled and ran toward her. "Think of the love surrounding you. Fight his magic with your own power."

Her mother's magical dust surrounded Belle, creating a warm tingly feeling.

"Fight him, Belle!" her dad shouted. "Dig deep into your heart. We love you too much to lose you again."

"Stop." G-Dad's magic froze her parents in place.

Belle struggled with the emotions swirling inside her. She wasn't strong enough to fight him. Her grandfather's magic held her captive, unable to think clearly.

"Don't let him take you? Fight him," her father screamed.

No way did she want to go with him, but she didn't have the strength.

She heard a motorcycle with the distinctive Knucklehead's sound as it rumbled to a stop.

"Lucky?" Had he really come?

His motorcycle revved as he pulled up along the curb. He took off his helmet, raked his finger through his dark hair, and gazed in her direction.

Hope surged through her. Even though she hadn't spoken to him in weeks, she hoped he still cared about her.

"What in tarnation is that noise?" her grandfather's fingers dug into her arms. G-Dad changed into his Cupid stature, but not her. "Why are you still mortal sized?" he growled.

"Because I'm half human." Just not strong enough to fight his magic. Her own magic must be multiplying G-Dad's like the legend's words had proclaimed.

CHAPTER 25

Women Lucky had dated in the past constantly checked their phones for messages or would take photos and post them on Instagram, Snap Chat, or who knows what else. He found it refreshing that Belle didn't buy into that nonsense. Until he walked away from her.

The only number he had belonged to her parents. A week ago, after he'd chilled out over the L bomb, he'd tried calling. It went to voice mail. No way would he leave a message on her folks' machine. He wanted to text her and see how things were going, wanted to talk to her, wanted to say he was sorry about the way he behaved.

The last few weeks, he had been miserable. Gran had no qualms about telling him to get off his ass and go after her.

He was pulling up to the house, determined to remedy

the hurt he'd caused, knowing he'd made a big mistake. She was worth fighting for.

He blinked several times. Belle was arguing with an older man. When he gripped her arm, Lucky jumped off his bike and ran toward the over-aged bully. "Take your hands off her." Nobody messed with his chick.

"I will do no such thing. We're leaving now." Wings unfurled from his shoulders, and the guy shrunk to be shorter than the front wheel of his motorcycle.

"What the hell?" Lucky's jaw dropped, and he stared at the scene playing out in front of him, watching the little guy levitate Belle off the ground. How was that possible?

"Use the power of love that's deep inside you to fight him," her mother screamed.

"Belle!" Lucky tried to reach for her ankles but couldn't connect.

Fear fired through his brain.

Without Belle, his life would be empty.

"I love you." The words slipped out. The realization hit him hard. He did love her. "I need you by my side."

"You really love me?"

"I know I freaked out." He was pretty freaked out about the crazy scene in front of him, but a little voice in his head said to keep talking or he might lose her forever. And that would be intolerable. "You're the smartest, sweetest, most beautiful lady I know. Are you going to let a little guy with wings get the better of you?"

"No, I'm not."

"Feel our combined power of love," her mother shouted. "Let it give you strength."

The heart emblem on her wrist sparkled brightly. "Love that comes from the heart trumps your power over me." Silvery dust swirled around her. As if an electrical current switched off. She plummeted into Lucky's arms.

"That's quite an entrance, princess." Lucky set her on the ground and held her. No wonder he found her so special. "Always knew there was something extraordinary about you." He brought his lips to hers. Warmth simmered through his soul.

The strange winged guy floated down a few feet from Belle. His dust swirled around her. "You can't fight destiny. You belong in Cupid's Corner."

"My destiny is to remain here."

"You're a ruthless bastard." Her mother rushed toward the flying guy, but he floated upward out of reach.

"You've got that right, mom," Belle said as Lucky held tight around her waist.

"I thought you were my special granddaughter." He flew above the group. "In reality, you are selfish."

"I feel sorry for you," Belle said. "You assumed my power would enhance Cupids within the Brook's family line. The DNA connection doesn't matter. My power comes from deep in the hearts of people who truly love me."

"She's right. Everyone here adores you, Belle, except for him." Her father pointed to the fluttering guy. "It's time to leave and never bother us again."

"Not without Belle."

"I've already proven my powers are now stronger than yours. Go back where you belong with your tail between your legs."

"Belle belongs in Cupid's Corner." Once again, dust circled around Belle. Nothing happened. The guy grunted.

"She belongs here," her mother snapped. "You had no right to abduct my child and deprive me and Troy of the chance to watch her grow up with her brother."

"I did it out of love, Zinnia. Raising a child with magical abilities wouldn't be easy on Earth." The guy fluttered several feet above them, pulled out a handkerchief from his suit pocket, and wiped his forehead.

"That's bullshit," Troy said, his hands fisted.

"Troy, let it go," Zinnia whispered.

"Fine, but if you ever show your face around here, you'll be greeted by the barrel of a gun." Her dad yelled.

"I'm not afraid."

"You should be, G-Dad. Maybe I should contact the council and explain what you did. You'll be ruined." Belle laughed.

He actually snorted, but his sullen expression showed worry.

"You're pathetic." She motioned to the clouds. "Leave now, or I'll sick a conspiracy of ravens to chase you."

"I'll be back." The guy flew off.

Lucky rubbed his eyes. "What just happened?" he whispered in her ear.

"Come with me." She grabbed his hand. "We need to talk."

LUCKY AND BELLE sat at a picnic table in the backyard. "I can't believe you came." She ran her fingertips along his cheek.

"I was miserable without you." Now that his adrenaline mode to protect had waned, he needed to understand what he saw. "Think you can explain what I witnessed out there. I take it you're related to the flying guy."

"I used to call that man grandfather until I learned he kidnapped me away from my real parents. Just so we're clear, I am also a Cupid from the heavenly realm above the cumulous clouds."

He looked up to a thin, wispy layer and further to the puffier formations. He attempted to make sense of the craziness. "Okay. You're a Cupid?"

"A hybrid. Half Cupid, half human." She crossed her gorgeous legs and jiggled her foot. "Does that matter?"

"It's different." The whole scene still confused him.

"If you can't handle this … us …" she said softly.

He wasn't sure what he could handle. "Does this mean you can fly?

"Um … yes."

Belle could fly. Crazy. Unbelievable. Actually fascinating.

"Say something, please. Tell me what you're thinking?" Her words came out clipped.

He pulled her onto his lap. Regardless of what she could do, he needed her close. “Relax, princess.”

She remained a bit stiff in his arms.

“Since your magical, whatever I wish for can come true, right?” This had possibilities.

“I’m not a genie.” She rolled her eyes.

Good. Annoyance was a marked improvement from wariness. “Then what can you do?”

“Nothing huge. Change shape. Fly. Create my own outfits, my next meal.”

“And fight off self-absorbed relatives who try to kidnap you—like a superhero.”

“There is that.” She scrunched her nose. “What else do you want to know about me?”

“You somehow can use magic, right? How does it work?”

“Basically, the magic is stored in my heart emblem. I get an image or idea in my head, and when I flick my fingertips, the dust comes out of the ends.”

“That’s incredible.” He traced his pointer finger over her wrist. An idea popped into his head. “Show me what you look like as a Cupid.”

“Are you sure?”

“Since I didn’t freak out seeing your grandfather fluttering around, I doubt I will when you change.”

She flicked her fingertips. Silvery-purple dust swirled around her, transforming her into a sixteen-inch fairy. She wore a violet gown that came to her knees and glittering translucent pink wings unfurled from her shoulders

"That's amazing." He stared at her.

She flew closer and kissed his cheek.

"What's it like to fly?"

"Hmm ... it's freeing, I guess."

"Wish I could join you." Flying looked exciting. "Think you could shrink me with your magic?"

"I can try." She swirled her dust, and he shrunk to the size of a magpie.

He checked behind his shoulder. "No wings."

"Hold still, and I'll try again." Her dust swirled around him and transformed him back into his regular size. "Sorry."

"Might be for the best. I'd probably fly into a pole or the side of a building." Getting used to her abilities would take some adjustment, but he'd figure this out.

She floated to the ground, transformed back to her regular size, and eased next to him. "I'm surprised you're okay with my magical abilities?"

"Don't mind as long as it comes with the rest of the package." He breathed in her floral scent. "You know, as a kid, Gran read me a story about a Cupid who fell in love with a mortal."

"Did the girl look like me?"

"Nope. She was an adorable blonde. Think you could dye your hair?"

She slapped his hand.

"Did you know your eyes darken when you're riled?" He ran his thumb along her chin."

'Why'd you freak out when I said I loved you? I assumed

you didn't love me back. You thought of me as a night's entertainment, a good time." Her eyes drifted to the ground.

He cupped his hands around her face and forced her to look at him. "We haven't known each other long. I was confused."

"You weren't the only one."

Elation filled him, and he couldn't help smiling. He loved Belle. He said the words earlier but under duress. Hell, she was floating several feet above him. But now he'd have to face the truth. What if her feelings had changed? He had to ask since she hadn't said the words earlier. "You love me, right?"

She looped her arms around his neck and initiated a heated kiss. "Does that tell you anything?"

"Not in words."

"I love you," she said softly.

"That's much better."

"I think there's more to why the three words bugged you."

He let out a deep breath. She deserved to know the truth. "Love hasn't worked out for me. My mom used to say she loved me, and then she ran away. My father became a drunk and literally clocked out of my life. My ex said she loved me but dumped me when I had my accident." He paused, attempting to compose his thoughts.

"None of that was your fault."

"I know. It took me a couple of weeks to realize I abandoned you because of fear. It was easier to walk away than to take a chance on rejection." He pulled her back onto his lap and brought his lips to hers. "When we were separated, all I could think about was the beautiful woman with auburn hair and violet eyes."

"Damn, you're good."

He wiped off a tear streaking her cheek. "I plan to show you just how good later on tonight."

"We'll see about that." Her sensuous tone said otherwise.

He snuggled closer and kissed her deeply.

Her bottom wiggled.

"We've got more things to discuss." He set her next to him.

"Like what?" She tensed.

"Where do we go from here? I live in a studio at the back of my grandmother's garage, and you're a two-hour drive away."

"I don't care where we live. I'll move in with you."

"Tried that once. It didn't last." He loved her too much to repeat that mistake.

"Then we'll commute to see each other."

"Or you could stay with Gran on the weekends and help out at the bar."

"Okay." She brushed her lips against his.

"Did you get the flowers I sent yesterday."

"Flowers?"

He got out his phone and searched his emails. "Dammit. I meant to send them yesterday."

"You're here, and you love me. Best present ever." She showed her love by giving him a searing kiss.

CHAPTER 26

Three months later, Lucky and Belle strolled along Tranquility Lake's trail holding hands. He tapped his jean pocket for about the fifth time as they reached the top of a hill overlooking the city.

"We haven't been here since that first weekend."

She looked gorgeous in black pants and a silver blouse. Her wavy hair was loose.

"Have a seat." He motioned to a bench and rocked on his heels, his mouth dry, his hands clammy.

"You're acting a little weird." She sat and tilted her head.

"Am I?" Holding her hand, he dropped onto his good knee. His injured knee smarted like heck, but that didn't stop him from reaching in his pocket and pulling out a black box, all the while gazing into her eyes. "I started falling for you when you took your frustration out on your shoe. You were freezing, without a dime to your name, and still debated whether to take my offer for a night in a warm room." He laughed. "Smart girl."

"You thought I snuck in the stockroom to steal. Yet, you wouldn't leave me alone." She fluttered her eyelashes.

"I hadn't seen you walk through the bar. How did you end up there?"

"It's pretty embarrassing."

He kissed the top of her hand. "But you're going to tell me?"

"I used an invisibility potion," she said like it was a normal everyday occurrence.

"You can become invisible?" He'd like to try that sometime.

"With a potion I'd found. I have no idea how to create one myself." She shook her head. "But knowing Serenity, she might figure it out."

"Did you knock down my bike?"

"Guilty. I should have slowed down on my landing. Anyway, I snuck to the side of the building, and my hand ran against my naked thigh. Something happened, and I found myself in my birthday suit."

"I like the picture."

"You would." She laughed. "I felt for my backpack, pulled on the dress, but I could only get my head and one arm in." She shook her head. "It so dumb."

"And when you went into the stockroom to fix it, you

didn't think to grab your backpack because it was invisible at the time."

"Exactly. The potion started wearing off when I walked by the restrooms."

"I think fate intervened. We were meant to be together." His bad leg now twinged. "Will you marry me?"

"Oh my gosh, yes." She stared at the box. "Isn't it customary to slip the ring on my finger?"

"You're pretty bossy." He couldn't stop grinning as he took the band out of the box and slipped in on.

"Perfect fit." She held up her hand, and the square-shaped diamond sparkled in the sunlight. "I can't believe you bought me a ring with the princess cut."

"It suits you." He moved to the bench next to her. It stunned him she'd accepted. "About the wedding, let's elope tonight?"

"No way. I want my dad and brother to walk me down the aisle."

"Figured you'd say something like that. We could get hitched at this park."

"Down by the river would be perfect. Our reception could be at the Rebel Rouser Tavern. It's always been a fantasy of mine to ride on the back of a Harley in a wedding dress."

"That can be arranged." He kissed her soft and tenderly.

She gazed at her ring sparkling in the sunlight and simpered. "I love my diamond."

"And me?"

"Not as much."

"Why'd I have to pick such a sassy fiancé?"

"Because I come in handy in the garage, and you find me irresistible."

"You are mighty tempting. About the shop?" he said. "I've been putting aside money and thought I'd have enough to start building next summer."

"You need me to pick up extra shifts at the bar to help out?"

"Not if the bar sells." He flashed her a smile. "Yesterday, we got an excellent offer. Geezer's more than ready to retire."

"Your dream will finally come true."

"Our dream. I need you by my side." He gazed into her beautiful violet eyes.

"Oh, Lucky," she said with a sigh.

"Along with building the shop, we should be able to put a hefty down payment on a house."

"I'm fine in the studio apartment."

Their plan for him to stay in Gran's spare room when she was in town, sleeping in his bed, lasted two weeks. It turned out, he loved waking up with her in his arms. "When we start having kids, we'll need more room." He thought for a second. "You do want kids, don't you?" He stared at her and imagined having a daughter with her pretty red hair.

"In a year or two. I need some alone time with you first." Her eyes got wide. "What if our cherub inherits my Cupid powers?"

"I'll love any child we have." He pushed a wayward hair behind her ear. "I love you."

"You're way too sweet."

"Shh. You'll ruin my hard-ass reputation."

"As if." She laughed. "About the house, when we need more space, maybe we could add on to your place. I like sharing the kitchen with Gran and Farryn. They're teaching me to cook, the old-fashioned way." She gave him an impish smile. "You did say I was a whiz at following directions."

"I did, didn't I." He kissed the top of her head.

"Did I mention I love you, Lucky O'Sullivan?"

"Not that I recall." He kissed her for the longest time. "Let's go to my place and start practicing for the honeymoon."

"After I call my mom and tell her I'm gonna be the rebel's Cupid." She pulled her phone out of her pocket.

Life with his Cupid would never be dull.

The End.

COWBOY'S CUPID

Cowboy's Cupid

If you enjoyed REBEL'S CUPID, you might want to read COWBOY'S CUPID from my Love's Magic Series.

A Forbidden Love

When Cupid's arrow accidentally strikes the wrong cowboy, she's supposed to fix her mistake—not fall for the alluring mortal.

Cami Calypso receives her first assignment just in time for the Valentine season. As a newbie Cupid Archer, her life is perfect until her arrow accidentally strikes the wrong man. She has sixty days to secure a job as his housekeeper on a ranch and find the cowboy his soul mate—not keep him for herself.

Rhett Holloway needs a housekeeper and cook.
He doesn't need an adorable blonde to distract him.
He doesn't need her to fix his love life.
But here she is, and he finds her irresistible.

Read an excerpt from COWBOY'S CUPID.

EXCERPT

Rhett had a strange feeling in his gut during dinner. Cami kept checking her watch. He'd asked what bothered her, but she said everything was fine.

After a long day, he helped her clean up the dinner dishes, and they walked to her apartment. Her stance was rigid, her body tense. She didn't shift toward him as he strode with his arm around her shoulder.

"What's wrong?"

"I need to tell you something." She shrugged but wouldn't look at him.

They'd only known each other close to two months, but his heart was all in. He unlocked the apartment door. Seated at the edge of the couch, Cami put a distance between them and avoided eye contact.

"Go ahead." He stood by the kitchen table and waited for a response.

"We were never meant to be together," she said, still not looking his way.

His chest hurt. She was breaking up with him.

"I've got a secret. When I show you, I hope you'll still love me."

"Whatever you've done in the past doesn't matter. We'll get through it." He'd made his share of mistakes.

She extracted a glass vial from her pocket. It sparkled and shimmered. "It's not what I've done, it's what I am."

"What are you?" He didn't even see a flicker of a smile.

Her lips tightened into a grimace. "Please listen carefully to what I say."

"All right. Spill." He tapped the side of his pants.

She licked her lips and took a deep breath. "I told you I was a Cupid when you brought me to the archery range."

"Okay."

She folded her arms. "I live in Zeus' Kingdom up in the clouds."

His teeth ground, as he sat next to her and said sarcastically, "Of course you do."

"You've seen my archery skills. Even said I was talented." She lifted her chin and blew out a breath. "I am a Cupid, a real live Cupid."

"That's crazy." Maybe she was crazy. His primal instinct told him to leave, but he couldn't move.

"My occupation is an archer." Tears pooled in her eyes. "I'm telling you the truth."

"If you're leaving me, say so, and quit making up this lame story."

"I don't want to go anywhere." She twirled a curl around her finger.

"You don't? And here I thought you were breaking up with me."

"If only things were different. I've got to return home." She looked at her watch.

"So, you are leaving me? Why?" He was confused.

"I don't want to. I'm happy here." Her shoulders slumped, her chin dropped. "My whole life I've dreamed of being good enough."

"But you are good enough." She was the best thing to ever happen to him. "You're perfect for me."

"Don't make me cry, please let me finish." Her eyes softened. "I've dreamed of visiting Earth and infusing humans with arrows of love. When I got my first earthly assignment, I hit the wrong man, namely you."

Those blue eyes. "You shot me with your arrow of love?"

"It was a mistake. My assignment ducked, and I hit you instead. I was sent to rectify my mishap and set you up with your soulmate. We were never supposed to fall in love."

"You love me." His spirits soared.

"Yes."

"'Bout time you admitted it." He moved closer, but she backed up, out of his reach.

"Will you accept the real me?"

"What do you mean? The real Cami's right in front of me."

"Watch." Rocking back and forth on her heels, her cheeks flushed to a rosier red.

His eyes riveted to her hands.

She unscrewed the glass vial and poured out a glittery substance. Iridescent pink dust swirled and surrounded her. Her body shrunk to the size of a doll, dressed in a shimmering gown. Iridescent wings formed at her shoulders. She flew up midway between the floor and the ceiling.

"Holy shit!" He stared, not frightened, confused.

"I'm a C-Cupid." Her words came out broken.

He froze, became immobile. "This can't be happening."

"I love you, always will." She hovered close to him, and he felt her lips kiss his cheek.

"It's unreal."

"Tell me about it." Her eyes were wide. Wary.

"You really are a Cupid?"

"Yes. Do you still love me?"

He didn't know what to think. "It's too much." He turned his back to her, put his head in his hands.

His girlfriend—a ruler-sized pixie. It couldn't be true.

Except he'd seen her.

If you enjoyed REBEL'S CUPID, here's a preview of the first chapter in FIREBRAND's CUPID, Love's Magic Series-Book Three

FIREBRAND'S CUPID

CHAPTER 1

The Realm of Cupid's Corner

On the outskirts of town, Zander Eros floated down to a grassy meadow near Aphrodite's Lake. He unfurled his wings, plucked a crooked feather, swirled his magical ruby dust from his fingertips, and turned his glittery sky-blue wings black. Black matched his cheerless mood. He peered over the edge of a cumulus cloud to Earth, guzzling from a bottle of Hennessy brandy brought from the world below. Taking a long swig, bitterness filled his thoughts—all because of his two-timing ex, Cami Calypso.

The little Cupid crushed their carefully laid plans, plans that originated when they were cherub neighbors. Their marriage was expected. The idea perpetuated by both the Eros and Calypso families. He and Cami were both attractive and exceptional marksman. They'd been deemed the Golden

Archers. Their children would be extraordinary, their life perfect.

Curse Cami for saying she never loved him. Curse her for choosing a *human* over him and marrying a cowboy just yesterday. Curse her father for giving his blessing. A sharp pain dug deep in his heart. Her father used to treat Zander like a son, but that would stop now that he wouldn't be a part of Cami's life. Fury blazed inside his mind as he polished off the last drop of brandy and propelled the bottled toward the lake. It hit a boulder near the shoreline and shattered into broken pieces—shattered much like his future.

Why had she worn his ring if she didn't want to marry him? Everyone in town knew about the engagement. Once word got out about her choosing a mortal, he'd be looked down on by society. His social standing would be in question. The concept made his stomach turn.

Cami *should* love *him*, not a *human*.

A message flashed on his wrist heart emblem.

Holy shit.

He had an Earthly assignment to complete. Two hours before sunset—on a Sunday, no less. His last assignment, and he'd have over a month off.

His head was a bit fuzzy. What did it matter? He'd been a champion archer since the age of ten and never missed a target on purpose. At least the task should be fast and easy. According to the couple's profile, they needed a love boost. Shooting arrows filled with a love potion when his own love life was in shambles. Hypocrisy at its finest. If only Cupids could receive love boosts. Cami would realize her mistake.

Once he fixed the doomed couple's relationship, then what? Since his best friend recently moved to Lover's Landing, he had nowhere to go. Nobody to hang with. Nothing to do except spend time with his new pal, Hennessy. While on Earth, he could easily find a bar or saloon in town and pretend to be a human for the night. He might as well drink where nobody knew him. Failing to snag the expected wife, he wasn't ready to face his community.

He flew above the dirt path through the Calypso Forest.

Calypso.

The forest named after one of Cami's ancestors.

He couldn't wait to get far away from this realm to regroup and figure out a new game plan. As he took the fork to the left away from the giant redwoods, a violet cuckoo perched on a branch. Its distinct call annoyed him like the cuckoo clock on the wall in his den.

Rays of light flickered on the Fates River. This sunbeam would take him to Moosehead, Idaho. He glided to the edge, opened his wings wide, and wrapped his arms around the radiant column. The speed sobered him.

Cursed chaos, he approached the hotel too fast.

Pushing his wings in close to his body, they failed to slow his descent through the roof of the Moosehead Lodge. He skidded to a stop on top of an oak mantle secured to a massive stone fireplace. The tips of his shoes tapped against a silver-framed photo. It wobbled precariously close to the edge and stopped.

Luckily, the two people behind the concierge counter were engrossed in their conversation and didn't look in his direction. Whew!

Wiping a bead of sweat from his brow, he breathed in deeply. Baked goods overrode the scent of pine. He glanced at the people seated on couches and chairs, across the shiny wooden floor to the customers on bar stools drinking. No amber-colored auras. No signs of a distressed couple. His assignment should be around here somewhere.

The front door swung open.

"If you loved me ..." a man's voice yelled from outside.

Bingo. He'd found the couple.

Now to recall the couple's file. He tapped his heart emblem on his wrist, pulled up a virtual screen, and skimmed the info.

Married for five years, the wife gave all her attention to their two kids. He felt neglected. This was their first time leaving the kids for a weekend.

The front door opened, allowing him to flutter outside under the veranda.

"You don't want a wife, you want a cook and housekeeper," a woman snarled.

Their love lights faded. A love boost would allow her to see that her husband longed for affection.

Time to complete his task. He took his quiver and bow

off his shoulder, snatched a silver arrow, nocked it in place, and floated lower.

The wife stood facing her husband with her hands on her hips. "I'm going to call the sitter."

Zander moved a few feet from her, saw the perfect angle, and released his arrow. Zing. Dark pink lit her heart.

"I love you. I miss holding you at night," the man said.

Her expression softened. "I miss you, too."

He pulled her into his arms, and they were kissing.

Success.

Normally, Zander would be overjoyed. Another tally to add to his chart, but today his completed task seemed flat. He flew to the side of the Moosehead Lodge to transform into his human size, floated to the ground, swirled magical dust from his fingertips, and his body grew larger. He flicked more dust and jeans and a golf shirt formed around him, followed by black Ralph Lauren loafers.

Across the street, lights from the Bison Tavern flashed and caught Zander's attention. A drink sounded perfect.

With dusk settling on the horizon, people continued taking selfies in front of a bison statue. Others ambled along the sidewalk in T-shirts or light sweatshirts. Not a bad place for vacationers out on a stroll.

A handful of vehicles parked in the slots lining the main street. Half a dozen cars passed by. A monster-sized truck pulled into a parking lot behind the back of the building.

Like it mattered how many mortals were around—he had nowhere important to go. Strolling across the street, he couldn't believe someone hung real antlers on the façade surrounding the Bison Tavern sign. He strode up planked steps, opened a squeaky door, walked into a long rectangular room, went up to the bar and squeezed in-between a couple of men in cowboy hats.

TIME TO SAVE A COWBOY

If you enjoyed REBEL'S CUPID, you might want to read TIME TO SAVE A COWBOY from my Western Romance Time Travel Series.

The Cowboy Doesn't Deserve to HANG

Captivated by the story of a cowboy hanged as a horse thief in 1890, Mia Kellogg travels back in time with only thirty days to save an innocent man.

Dusty Mann is determined to buy his own ranch.

He doesn't need a modern, straightforward woman to barrel into his life or knock his plans off track.

But Mia steals his heart—and then says she's from the future.

Read an excerpt from TIME TO SAVE A COWBOY

EXCERPT

In front of Mia, a gentleman in a dark suit and top hat assisted a lady into her carriage seat. The driver positioned himself to her left and picked up the reins. His horse neighed.

Mia shifted back a few steps, giving the horse plenty of room as she leaned her elbows against a railing behind her. The buggy took off leaving thin ruts in the powdery dirt.

Hot air raced down her neck. Something hit the back of her head, jerking her forward, pushing her, making her stumble into the street. She gained her footing. Spun around. Her arms pinwheeled. “Stop tha—”

Her words clogged her throat, cut off her breath.

A horse, oh no, a horse.

She stared at its large, triangular brown head inches from

her face. No, not large. Gigantic. Her heart tripped in her chest; her legs became immovable.

Its nostrils flared, its obsidian-colored eyes widened.

She tried to move, but her limbs became rigid, her feet cemented in place. The horse stomped one hoof against the ground and swished its tail against its flank. A thousand pounds of imposing beast sniffed the air.

She stood frozen, watching its nostrils flair and flatten, flare and flatten. "Get, get back."

The horse's mouth opened, and it bared teeth the size of playing cards.

Move, she told herself. Move, before it stomps on you.

The horse let out a high-pitched snort and threw its head up.

She was gone, racing down the street, sprinting up the hotel's wide wooden staircase, straight through an open door, running fast. Fear propelled her like a slingshot.

She charged inside and plowed into a solid object with an umph.

"Slow down." Large hands steadied her and released its hold. The man stepped away.

At only five-foot-two, she stared straight at his massive shoulders. This guy must spend hours at the gym. Okay, she had to quit gawking at his chest. She gazed up as he took off his worn-leather Stetson.

He gave her a lopsided grin. "Somethin' troubling you?"

"No." Not wanting to seem like an idiot, she stoned her expression, while her knees wobbled.

"You're kinda pale. Best you sit a spell." He placed his hands on her shoulders and guided her to an overstuffed couch near a brick fireplace. Heat sizzled through her gown's fabric, and her insides tingled.

"Excuse me." The cowboy flagged a waitress in a long black dress and white apron. "I'd be obliged if you brought this lady some water." He relaxed in an adjacent armchair and flashed her a brazen smile. "Never had a beautiful gal barrel into me. What's the hurry, miss?"

"Um, you see, this horse, it scared me. The horse, um, was huge, enormous." Sounding stupid, she concentrated on a multicolored glass-blown vase on the side table and rearranged the orange poppies to be in front of the violets and lupines.

"Must've been one of Ben's Belgian draft horses," he said, and she noticed his russet brown hair touched the top of his shirt collar.

The server handed her a glass of water. She took a sip. "It's warm."

"No surprise. This is the desert." The cowboy's drawl didn't seem practiced.

"I'm not as freaked as—" She looked at him, really looked at him, and recognized those wide-set gray eyes from somewhere. "You look familiar."

"I'd remember meeting a pretty gal like you." His smile lit up his handsome face, and her heart fluttered.

She focused on the people at the front desk. A clerk slid a

key to a man, and he left with a lady in a long chiffon dress. Most likely people from the train.

A heavy-set woman approached her. "I'm Jenny Hayes. My husband, Bob, and I manage the hotel."

"Mia Kellogg." She held out her hand.

Jenny gave her a sideways glance.

Why wouldn't she shake her hand? Must be a germaphobe.

"Saw Dusty walk you in. Did the heat get to you?"

"Maybe a little. I'm fine now." Mia examined his features. His tan complexion set off his wolf gray eyes. He was a ringer to the cowboy from the picture in the antique shop. "Your name's Dusty?"

He straightened and rewarded her with a mischievous grin. "Yep."

"His given name's Harold Mann, but folks have been calling him Dusty since he was knee high to a grasshopper." Jenny butted in. She must be related to him somehow. "What brings you to our town?"

"A short vacation."

"Well, you certainly chose an ideal time for your stay. Tomorrow's our monthly ball." Jenny's cheeks reddened.

Now Mia was confused. She and Birdie had tickets for the Daggett dance. Maybe she got the name of the town wrong. Still, if her relatives were here, she should have seen them by now. "Could I borrow your phone and call my cousin?" Mia asked, anxious to talk with someone she knew.

"Golly, we don't have a telephone here. Our general store

is the only business in town that has one. The shop's closed 'till morning," Jenny said.

Mia's throat got tight. Only one phone in town. This took the turn-of-the-last-century thing a bit far.

"I imagine you're famished, miss. May I find you a table in the dining room?"

"Please." Starved, at least her stomach didn't rumble.

Jenny turned to Dusty. "Will you be joining Miss Kellogg?"

Mia expected him to refuse politely. Not say, "I'd be honored." He stood and offered his arm. His scent of leather and masculinity made her lean closer. Wrong response for a guy she'd just met.

Jenny led the two of them through the spacious ballroom. Mia's right foot hit a slick, polished spot on the hardwood flooring. "Oh no."

Dusty tightened his grasp on her arm. "Careful, darlin'."

Was her lightheadedness from lack of food or … was it him? She took small mindful steps to their linen covered table. Mindful of the waxed floor. Mindful of clutching his muscular biceps.

"Here you go." He pulled out her chair. His gray eyes darkened when he looked at her. He appeared well-mannered, but she wondered if his kisses would hold a bad boy edge. She couldn't believe she thought about kissing him. Not exactly appropriate for a guy she barely knew—but he was cute.

Her eyes drifted to the five-o'clock shadow on his chin.

Certain she'd been caught staring, she unfolded her napkin and placed it on her lap.

“Enjoy your meal,” Jenny said and scurried off.

Mia should be looking for her phone, but hunger won out. She knifed jelly on a roll and bit into the warm orange-flavored dough. Wickedly scrumptious. She drank from a crystal glass. “The lemonade’s sour.” A pound of sugar wouldn’t take away the tartness.

He held up a crystal bowl. “Want some sugar?”

“Please.” She should use Sweet’N Low but being on vacation why not splurge a little? She added three generous teaspoons, deciding she’d make up for her indulgences at spin class on Monday. “What do you do?”

“Do?” His brow rose, and he looked at her like she asked him to explain the theory of relativity.

“Your job.”

“Me? I’m a cowhand.” His drawl came out a bit over exaggerated.

Her dad regularly watched old westerns. This guy had a casual Gary Cooper presence. She focused on the jagged scar on his chin. She liked the flaw, showed he wasn't plastic-perfect. “Where's your ranch?”

“It’s not mine.” He winced for a flash. “I’m the foreman of Los Flores Ranch.”

The hot cowboy sitting across from her lived in the next town over. Moving back to her hometown suddenly had a big advantage, namely him. She could see him working on the ranch on the outskirts of Hesperia. Lifting bales of hay would explain his beefy arms.

She'd have to give him her number before she left.

<u>TIME TO SAVE A COWBOY</u>

BOOKS

Romance Novels by Niki Mitchell

COWBOY'S CUPID

TIME TO SAVE THE COWBOY

REBEL'S CUPID

TIME FOR LOVE

FIREBRAND'S CUPID

LOVE'S HIGH TIDE

Children's Books by Niki Mitchell

KURIOUS KATZ

KURIOUS KATZ AND THE BIG MOVE

KURIOUS KATZ AND THE PLAY DAY

KURIOUS KATZ AND THE NEW FRIEND

KURIOUS KATZ AND THE BIRTHDAY PARTY

KURIOUS KATZ AND THE HALLOWEEN COSTUMES

KURIOUS KATZ AND THE CHRISTMAS TREE
KURIOUS KATZ AND THE BEST CHRISTMAS EVER
FOSTER CATS: ARTEMIS AND HER SNEAKY BROTHER HERCULUES
KURIOUS KATZ AND THE FOURTH OF JULY
KURIOUS KATZ AND THE VALENTINE SURPRISE
KURIOUS KATZ AND THE SNICKERDOODLE STORY

COMING SOON
PRECIOUS PUPS: BREEZY, THE LABRADOR RETRIEVOR

Niki Mitchell writes children's books along with contemporary fantasy and historical time-travel romance. She was born in Chicago, Illinois, and moved to Whittier, California in first grade. With a houseful of books and a local library located a few short blocks, her love of reading began at a young age.

Married for over thirty years and a romantic at heart, she enjoys writing about strong female characters in unusual settings. When she isn't playing with her cats, she loves reading, taking walks, water aerobics, photography, and traveling.

LINKS FOR NIKI MITCHELL

Dear Readers,

Thank you for reading REBEL'S CUPID.

I hope you enjoyed my story as much as I enjoyed writing it. Won't you please consider leaving a review? Even just a few words will help others decide if the book is right for them.

Best regards and thank you in advance.

Niki J. Mitchell

I look forward to hearing from my readers.

Visit me at https://nikimitchell.weebly.com/

Follow me on FaceBook at author Niki J. Mitchell

Twitter: Niki Mitchell@NikiMitchell7

Instagram: NikiJMitchellAuthor

www.ingramcontent.com/pod-product-compliance
Lightning Source LLC
Chambersburg PA
CBHW030354310726
48979CB00001B/304

* 9 7 8 1 9 5 1 5 8 1 2 4 4 *